THE LIFE OF MALÉ, a Horse

by

Sabrina J Ballentine

DEDICATION
To Jane Elliott and Trophy
Forever in your debt

"If we see cruelty or wrong that we
 have the power to stop,
and do nothing,
we make ourselves
sharers in the guilt."

Anna Sewell

6

Acknowledgements

My sister Cheryl, Keir and Nye.
Rebecca, for friendship like no other.

Amy Mitchell at Heavenly Hooves Equine
Podiatry for making so many dreams come true,
and all the members at the Happy Healthy Horse
Connection for their inspiration, skill and
friendship.

Dave, my heart horse, who taught me everything
I needed to know.

Destiny, Grace, Ant and Dec, and all the others.
I'm sorry for getting it wrong and you all helped
me get it right. Thank you for your patience. I
learn slow.

Russell Whitfield, for leading the way and
making me think it might just be possible

To the source of all things for showing me the
place where heart and heaven meet, That's where
the magic happens.

Contents

The Meadow

The sun stirs and with it every living thing in the meadow. Sunbeams fall through the leaves on the tree under which I lie and touch my face. I slowly open my eyes and see a bird in the canopy above. He calls to his mate and flies off to join her. Insects whirr and pass by on their busy way. The air is sweet with summer dew and the scent of grass and wild flowers.

I lift my head and see my friend, Joe, standing close by. His head held low, his eyes half closed, he seems to smile. He turns his head to touch me and I feel his warm breath for a moment before I get to my feet. With a yawn and a stretch, I look towards the gate just up the slope a short stroll from our favourite tree.

Soon Jemma will appear. She comes to see us every day. She brings us treats and strokes our heads and speaks softly to us, calling our names and asking how we are. I think she loves us very much. I am not sure why, because Joe and I are too old to carry anyone on our backs any more. No more rosettes or shiny silver cups. Jemma does not seem to care. She loves us anyway. It is enough that we carefully take from her cupped hands the treats she brings and lick her face and blow softly into her hair so she laughs and presses her cheek against us and stretches her arms around our necks. Jemma is not like other girls. The other girls consider her strange, but to us, she is a beautiful person who shines like the sun and lights up the cold dark days of winter.

When she first came to see us, she was a little shy and stood back from the fence so we had to stretch out our necks to reach the treats she held in her palms. But soon, she lost her fear and told us all about her life. About the children who stole her things and pushed her over and called her names until she cried. Joe and me listen and nudge her gently to remind her she is with us and she is safe.

It was not always like this. Joe and I have done many things. Our journey has been a long one and there was a time the horse box we travelled in was brightly decorated with rosettes, every colour of the rainbow, and silver cups jostled with each other on the mantlepiece until last year's were put aside to make way for the new. Then we were heroes! Our strength and speed and courage made us stand out from the crowd.

But time catches up with everyone, and we, like those before us, were moved aside to make way for the new, the younger, the fitter. So now we rest.

Birth

When daylight came my mother lifted her head from the straw in her stable to look at me. I shook my head, as all newborn foals do, to clear my ears of the water which had supported me as I grew but which now made way for the cool air and the arrival of many new sounds. The girl who watched over us wiped my face and rubbed my short wet fur with a rough towel. She seemed pleased and smiled as she stroked my mother's neck and spoke softly to her. I began to struggle to my feet, driven by a new hunger I scarcely understood. These legs are so long! I fall back into the straw and shake my head again. My mother pays me no attention. She lies still on the straw. The girl frowns. She sees the thick red blood seeping onto the straw from my former home.

'Oh no." She murmurs. "Please no...." and she rushes through the stable door shouting 'John.. John... Meg's bleeding... John..." Her voice fades as she runs to the farmhouse.

Then it was all a blur as people came and went. I never saw my mother again. She had been here many times before, but this time was the last.

The Field

Today it feels warmer, and the air tastes of blossom and grasses. I lick my lips and whicker gently to the mare who has become my mother. She lifts her head from the hay she is eating and turns to look at me. She too sniffs the air, then she turns towards the half door and looks out onto the fields. She drops her head to lick my shoulder.

"Today I believe we shall be allowed out."

"Out?" I ask. What is 'out'?"

"Into the fields, where the grass grows. It's getting warmer and you are now strong enough to run and play with the other foals. Soon you will eat the grass too."

"I won't! It looks horrid."

"Oh, you will. The grass is sweet and it will make you grow tall and strong. Until you are ready to leave me and stay with your new friends."

"Leave you? I shall never leave you! Why would I want to do that? I like it here with you."

She smiled and seemed sad for a moment as she gazed out over the stable door towards the fields. Then she nuzzled me and I drank my fill as we waited.

And it was not long before one of the girls came to give my mother her food and check her over as she did every day. This girl is my favourite as she always speaks quietly to me, strokes my face and rubs my ears. She laughs as I twist my head so she can tickle my chin. She tells me I am handsome and how much I have grown. My mother watches us while she eats her food, chewing slowly and savouring each mouthful. The girl offers me a tiny bit in her hand from my mother's bucket. I lick her hand and shake my head as the strange taste floods my mouth, the tiny pieces fluttering to the ground onto the pale straw.

"Maybe tomorrow, little man?" the girl says as she takes my mother's bucket to rinse it out ready for the next day, bolting the stable door behind her.

Then the big day came when we were to go out. The sun was shining after some rain and everywhere looked bright and fresh with the cobbles reflecting the sun's rays. I blinked as my eyes adjusted, following my mother out of our stable home to the gate at the end of the yard. In the fields either side were lots of other horses. On one side there were some more mares, each with their foals nearby, and on the other, some older foals in a group together. One of the mares whinnied to my mother, and she answered and trotted over to greet her as we were led through the gate. I followed closely. This world was so big! Enormous trees with hard brown trunks, grass with tiny yellow flowers and big blue skies with white clouds. I marveled at all of it, staying close to my mother as she walked with the other mares to the drinking trough, the shade of the tree or the gate to get her food each day. I watched the other foals run and jump and play chase with each other. Sometimes they fell over when their feet hit a stone in the ground, and their mother would whinny, concerned in case they were hurt, but they always got up again, shaking the dust from their coats, running to catch up with their friends who had raced on ahead of them.

But slowly, it all became familiar and homely, and I ventured a small distance from my mother's side. One day I caught sight of a small flying fluttering creature. It came to rest on a flower right next to me, and as I lifted my head and stretched my neck to sniff it, it flew away. I ran after it as it flew crazily up and down, back and forth, but then it went too high, way out of reach, and when I turned around, I could not see my mother at all. I stood fixed to the spot, not knowing what to do. I had never been without my mother before, her comforting presence was everything to me. I whinnied in panic, searching the field for her familiar shape, and then I heard her whinny back and saw her trotting over to me, her face full of concern. The other mares looked on as we greeted each other like long lost friends.

"What were you doing son?" she asked, as she licked my neck.

"I was chasing the fluttering flying creature, and when it flew too high, I was so far away I couldn't see you, and I was afraid."

"There is nothing to be afraid of here in the field. We are both safe. And I am never far away. It's time you played more with the other foals. It will help you when the time comes. Let's go and speak to Ace. She will know what to do."

I did not have chance to ask her what she meant about the time, but Ace, the mare who is in charge said I should make friends with Joe. He would help me be confident in the big world. Our mothers stood by whilst Joe and I looked at each other.

Joe seemed to know I wasn't very confident and he suggested we should go for a walk together, just to the big tree, and back again. Ace agreed and Joe set off and I stood for a moment watching his brown tail swinging as he walked, until my mother nudged me, and I followed after Joe, down the slope to the big tree in the middle of the field.

"This is my favourite tree," he said.

"Your favourite? Why?" I asked.

"Because in the summer, the leaves grow down so low you can eat them. And when it rains, if you stand underneath it, you don't get your coat wet. And when the sun is hot, and you've been running around, if you stand underneath it, you soon feel cool."

"That seems a very helpful tree."

Joe laughed. "I suppose it is" he said, "a very helpful, useful tree."

Some of the older foals were watching us and Joe said we should go back to our mothers as that was enough wandering for one day.

The next day I played with Joe from when we were let out of our stable in the morning, until the sun went down and we were taken back inside again for the night. I tried to copy everything Joe did. I even tried to nibble the grass and the low growing leaves on the hawthorn tree, like he did, but the grass took too long to chew and the tree had thorns so you had to be very careful when picking off the leaves.

One day, when Joe and I were playing at the bottom end of the field the older foals followed us and gathered round, pushing and shoving each other. The tallest foal seemed to be in charge and he spoke before all the others. He said that my mother wasn't really my mother. She had a foal already but they took it away from her so she could be my mother instead.

"Where did they take the other foal?" I asked.

"Oh, they killed it, of course" the older foal replied.

"Don't listen to him Malé," Joe said, "he doesn't know that happened."

"I do." The foal said. "I saw."

"What did you see?" I demanded. This was something I had not heard before. I vaguely remembered them taking my mother away and my new mother being brought to the stable next to me. She was warm and friendly and reached through the wooden bars and sniffed me for a while, then licked my damp fur, and then we shared a stable. But it was so long ago, and I was just a newborn foal.

"They took her foal away on a lorry. I saw."

Several of the other foals agreed that they had seen it too.

"It wasn't alive because they carried it."

I turned and ran. Away from the foals, and Joe. I ran to my mother.

"Mother, that foal said they took your foal away so you could be my mother. Is it true? Why did they do that? Mother...?"

I stopped as my mother suddenly looked sadly at me. Her big brown eyes shone. Joe caught up and stood beside Ace, who looked on as my mother spoke.

"Yes, it is true. Some of us mares have foals which are not as valuable as you, so they took mine away."

"But why?" I cried. "I don't understand!"

My mother patiently tried to explain. "You are the son of a very famous and valuable sire. Your mother worked as a show jumper and the humans wanted her foals to do the same. They chose that horse to be your father so that when you grow, you can do the same work that your mother did. Perhaps even better."

"But your foal... why was he not allowed to live?"

"Because... because his father was not so special and neither am I. So my foals are not as valuable as you. You needed a mother of your own so you could be cared for and thrive. But don't fret, son. It is the way of the world. And at least I have you."

Ace moved silently forward until she stood beside my mother. They hung their heads in silent grief.

"Joe?" Ace spoke quietly. "Take Malé to the gate please. It is nearly time for our food. Listen! The humans are preparing it now."

Joe put his head over my neck briefly as we made our way back up the field to the gate.

Lessons in Life

The days went along happily enough. During daylight, we spent our time running and playing, jumping over obstacles, some which no-one else could see, dozing in the warm sun, sleeping, eating the bright green grass and growing strong. Joe was born a month before me, and when we first became friends, he was taller and broader than I was. But now, we are about the same height. I can run as fast as any foal in our field. These long legs carry me past every one of them when we race all the way up the hill, pretending we have seen monsters in the stream or the hedge.

Our mothers scold us when we disturb their dozing, running too fast and too close, or round and round like the weather vane on the top of the clock tower. Sometimes the older foals tease Joe and me, and move us away from the best patch of grass, or the juiciest plants with their ears pinned back and their necks stretched. We laugh and run away, but I am careful not to run so fast that Joe is left behind.

My mother is not the same as the other mares. Her coat is brown and white and she is more heavily built. The others are plain colours. Even though she did not give birth to me, I love her more than anything.

One day, the biggest foal, a colt called Magic, was looking for a fight. Perhaps he was bored with our field and tired of the same old games. He ran up beside Joe and me as we stood by the stream watching the sunlight dancing, listening to the soothing sound as the water went on its merry way out of our sight.

23

"Look at you two daydreamers!" Magic sneered. "I think it's time you learnt who is the boss around here." And he turned his back end towards us and aimed a kick at Joe's ribs.

"Run!" I shouted, and we set off at a gallop, me in front with Joe close behind. Magic came after us. I went out in front, and then I saw Magic open his mouth to bite Joe's side. Anger flooded through me. Joe is my Friend! How dare you! In two short strides I dropped back to put myself between Joe and Magic. Magic swerved to avoid a collision, lost his footing and somersaulted over the grass to lie winded and panting. His mother ran over to him.

"My son, are you OK? What happened? What did they do to you?" Magic struggled to his feet and stood, sides heaving, beside his mother as she fussed over him. Magic glared at Joe and me. His mother, following his gaze, suddenly charged towards us, neck outstretched, teeth bared. Joe and me were fixed to the spot. We had not seen any of the mares do this before. All we could do was stare at her, holding our breath as her presence bore down upon us. I closed my eyes. In a flash, there was my mother, by my side, right in the way of Magic's mother and her huge white teeth and angry white rimmed eyes. Her teeth bared as she reared and squealed. Joe ran to his mother, and all the mares anxiously called to their foals, who ran to their side as if pulled by an invisible cord.

Ace saw and pushed through the group of mothers and their frightened foals banded together in a milling whirlpool of horses.

"Stop!" she said. "Stop it! What is happening here?"

"Her son pushed my son over!"

"He did not!" My mother protested. "Your son was about to bite Joe. He is just a foal and smaller than yours. You should teach him some manners!"

And so it went on for a short while until Ace lost patience.

"Stop it, both of you! I will take charge of Magic until he learns to behave. We cannot have our foals hurting each other. They must learn to play without harming anyone."

My mother hung her head and I did too. I had not intended to hurt anyone. But I could not let Magic hurt Joe.

Ace walked Magic and his mother to the gate away from the rest of us, and for the next two days she kept a close eye on them both.

Everything seemed to be calm again, under Ace's watchful eye, but my mother and Joe's stayed a little closer to us than before. It meant we didn't get so much chance to play rough games or race about quite so much, but it did mean we began to hear some things which didn't make us happy.

Ace was the oldest mare on the farm, and she had had many foals in her time. The last one had been difficult for her, as it was so large and for a while Ace was quite weak, so the humans decided enough was enough and Ace was not sent to the stallion again. Her back was swayed and her belly rounded after all those foals, but her eyes were kind. She was kept on to be the wisest mare, making sure all the mothers were well, and all the foals well behaved. The younger mares were shown how to discipline their foals, and what to do when they felt tired. Ace would show them where all the best plants grew to sooth aches and pains, making sure they ate properly and watched over them while they slept. We all loved Ace. The big world didn't seem quite so scary with our mothers and Ace around.

As we grew, we relied more on the sweet green grass in our field, and on the dry food the humans brought every day. I think our mothers were glad to see us growing strong as then they had to make less milk for us to drink, and soon they would be sent to the stallion again for their next foal in the Spring.

One day my mother told me that, since it was nearly Autumn time, I would be moved away from her and the other mares to live in the next field with all the foals that had been born that year. At first I didn't believe her, but Joe told me that his mother had said the same thing. I didn't like this idea, as I thought I should stay with my mother forever. She had taken care of me when my own mother died and I loved her more than anything, even Joe. I couldn't imagine not being able to stand by her side, sheltering when the wind blew, or feel her friendly nuzzles, or see her cross face when I was running around being annoying, which soon returned to gentle when I did as I was told.

It happened one cool day when the leaves were turning to red and yellow and brown all by themselves. Our favourite tree was so pretty, until the leaves began to fall, and then it started to look quite bare.

Ace was led through the gate first and turned out into the field next to the one we had always been in during the day. There she waited as each mare had her halter put on and was led to the field with her foal following. After a short while, when the foal was distracted, the mare was led away and the gate shut behind her. Most of them realized all of a sudden, that their mother had gone and they whinnied loudly, calling for the horse who had cared for them all of their short lives. The mothers whinnied back, and some trotted along the fence which separated them from their foal. Some of the foals ran to Ace and hid behind her, unsure of what to do next. Soon, all the foals were in the next field with Ace. She walked calmly down the field right to the bottom, followed by a bunch of bewildered-looking foals, and slowly back again. Some of the foals realized their mothers were not far away, just the other side of the fence, and settled down to eat the grass. Others whinnied and paced up and down. Ace followed them, encouraging them to eat, reminding them their friends were still there, and it was all going to be OK.

I stayed close to Joe, unable to think, almost unable to breathe. What if Magic began to torment us again? Where would I go to shelter if my mother's warm presence was no longer there? Who would comfort me when I was hurt? I didn't eat my food that evening, and Joe left some of his. As darkness fell, Joe and me stayed close to each other, gazing over the fence to where we used to be.

When the morning came, with the pale Autumn sunshine lighting up the dew on the grass, the mares were all returned to the field to graze and I ran along the fence until I saw my mother. She came over and licked my nose, just like she always did.

"Son," she said, "it will not be long before I will be taken back to the winter field. We may never see each other again. But always remember how much I love you. Try your best to please the humans, and life will be easier for you."

I could think of nothing to say but I knew that what she had said was true. All the foals had been told the same by their mothers. Ace did her best to prepare us all. But at that moment an ache was born in my heart which never goes away.

Out in the fields

As Autumn turned to Winter, the winds blew cold and heavy grey clouds blotted out the sun. The days grew shorter and the rain came down making the ground soft under our feet. Before the ground turned to mud we were taken in an enormous horsebox to a bigger field with a barn at one end which had straw spread on the floor for us to lie down on and hay in long wooden racks for us to eat. This was our winter home.

Our coats grew thick and woolly, and made us all look the same. I could always spot Joe – he was redder than most of us and had a long white blaze from between his eyes right down to his nostrils. Although I was born a little later than most of the others, I had already grown to about the same size, although my legs were longer. How I loved to run! No-one challenged me to a race any more, as they knew they would never be able to run faster than me. It felt good to stretch my slender legs as far as I could with every stride, feel my heart pound in my chest and my lungs fill with cold, clean air. Nothing stopped me when I galloped. I just jumped straight over anything in my way. Sometimes it felt like I could fly!

One day when the humans brought our food, there was another man with them. We crowded into the barn together, jostling for a place at the rack, our warm breath filling the cold air with mist. The man watched all of us eating, discussing us with the other humans, commenting on how well grown we were, how thick our coats, how well we all moved, how much some of us had taken after our fathers. This human pointed me out and asked if I was the one who had been orphaned at birth.

"Yes," the girl who fed us answered, as she threw an armful of hay into the rack. "He's Meg's foal, by Meadow Valley Dancer. He's going to be a star one day."

"I can see that," the man answered, "with legs like that I wouldn't be surprised if he could outrun his sire already!"

"He'll be staying here when the others go into training. John wants to keep him here and train him up for Fiona to ride."

"So he's not for sale then?"

"I wouldn't think so," the girl answered. "Fiona cried for a week when she lost Meg. John was quite worried about her for a time. That little chap is all they have left of her. All her other foals were snapped up straightaway. And with Dancer as his father he could go right to the top."

"Yes. He could," the man agreed, "that was a sad business with the mare," and then he asked about Joe and Magic and a grey filly called Grace.

Once we were all fed our buckets were cleared away into the pickup and the racks were all topped up for us to eat during the night. The man gazed at me for a while, and I looked back at him, slowly chewing on the sweet dry hay. That night I pondered the future and thought of my mother.

The days passed pleasantly enough. During the short daylight hours we grazed in the field, sheltering in the barn when the rain came down or the winds blew and filled our ears with noise. Joe and me spent most of our time together. Joe always seemed to be able to see the good in everything, nothing bothered him much. We looked out for each other, as we always had. Even Magic seemed to have settled down and did not trouble us at all.

One day we were separated into two groups, all the colts on one side, and the fillies on the other. I am not sure what happened, but one by one, the colts were taken into the stable across the yard where a man gave them something to make them sleep. The air smelt of the overpowering pink liquid the humans put on our skin when we cut ourselves with a thorn, and of blood.

When it was Joe's turn I tried to go with him, anxiously pushing my way past the girl at the gate and trotting loose round the yard until someone caught my halter and took me back towards the gate again.

"Oh, you're next then, are you?" the man said to me.

"No, not that one" one of the girls told him. "That's Meg's foal. He's staying entire."

"Ah, yes," the man replied. "If any of them are going to keep their balls, it ought to be him. A fine horse and no mistake."

I paced and whinnied and pawed the ground. The girls talked to me and tried to give me a treat from their pockets to calm me. I ignored them and stood watch by the gate and then breathed a sigh of relief when, several hours later, Joe was returned, walking slowly, a little shaky, but still the same Joe.

When the colts woke up, they had been gelded so that they could not father any foals. For a while, most of them were quiet and even Joe seemed bewildered. I stayed by his side and made sure he ate to keep his strength up.

After a few days, when the humans kept a closer eye on us than usual, their pain had gone, and life returned to normal. Except for Magic. It seemed that his operation had not gone well and, on the fourth day, he lay in the straw with his eyes half closed, sometimes groaning quietly. He did not eat or drink. Joe and Grace stood watch over him, and when the girls came to check on us in the pickup, Grace whinnied and ran to the gate to tell them Magic was ill and needed their help. The older girl called back to the farmhouse.

"John, it's the dark bay, Magic. He's down and not looking good." They spoke for a while in worried voices and then the girl got a blanket from the pickup and covered Magic until the other humans arrived. The man who had done the operations drove onto the yard, stopping quickly, spraying mud from his wheels, slamming his door and taking his bag from the boot, pulling on his long green overall as he walked. He stooped over Magic, folded back the blanket and listened to his heart and took his temperature. He asked the girls some questions, then he got some bottles from his bag and held them up so the liquid went into Magic's neck.

"You'll need to watch him overnight," the man said "and try to get him up as soon as you can. The more he moves the better. I'll come back to give him some more antibiotics in the morning."

"He's going to be OK though?" one of the girls asked.

"Probably," he replied. "It's an infection, but we've caught it early so I expect he'll be fine in a couple of days. Keep him warm and quiet. Can you move him away from the others, but within sight? We don't want him getting stressed on his own. Offer him some soft food as soon as he's on his feet."

The girls nodded, their lips pressed tightly closed as they glanced at each other. They didn't believe the man any more than we did.

Magic did not get to his feet that night. Nor the next day. On the third day his breath came in short rasps, each one an effort. The girls took it in turns to hold his head, stroking his neck beneath the thick blanket. Grace stood watch by the gate. She could just see into his stable if she stood right at the corner of the barn. Then, when the weak winter sun was highest in the sky, we heard the girl sobbing as if her heart would break. Grace took one last look, then walked slowly back to Joe and me at the hay rack with her head low. We ate in silence. There was nothing we could do.

***

The mood of our little group did not improve very much until the Springtime. We ate our food each day and spent many hours munching on the hay and sleeping in the straw in the barn. But Spring is when the sun returns and then the grass begins to grow again. It is sweet and lush, and it seems we can't eat enough of it. The big van came to take us to our Summer field, and we all stood swaying as we travelled just for a short while. Soon the van's engine stopped, the side door was opened and we blinked in the sunshine. Two of the girls got down from the front of the van to open the tall back door. The girls made sure we did not rush, and we all slowly and carefully stepped down the ramp onto the earth floor of the pen at the entrance to the new field. We all milled about, sniffing the fresh air and shaking our heads as the smells of new grass, leaves, flowers and the rich brown earth under our feet filled our nostrils, blown by the March wind. Several of the yearlings snorted and Grace stood on her hind legs, tossing her mane, impatient and eager to be out where the grass grew.

"Stand back, Soph, I'm opening the gate," the older girl said. The other girl ducked through the fence out of the way.

It was a good job that she did, since as soon as the gate was opened, there was a rush of horses in full gallop within 3 strides, a blur of brown and black and grey, running up the open field in joyful abandon.

Sophie laughed. "You weren't wrong there!" she said.

"Well, they are racehorses!"

After our first break for freedom, when we ran right round the perimeter fence, chasing each other, weaving in and out, bucking and rearing, Joe and me stood under the trees for a while, sampling the bright green leaves on the lower branches. Then we joined Grace and some of the others at one of the water troughs. The water was fresh and cold, and when a few of us drank from it at the same time, it made a hissing noise while it filled itself up again. The hedges all around were full of birds busily making nests, always twittering to each other. Soon we settled down to eat the grass. And how sweet and delicious it was! There was plenty of space in this field, and Joe and me often left the herd to talk quietly away from everyone else.

As the weather began to warm, the girls would come to feed us as they always did, but this time, one by one, our halters were put on, we were brought into the pen by the gate and each of us had lessons in how to walk calmly at the end of the rope, to give up each foot to have the mud cleaned out and to stand quietly to have the mud brushed from our coats. The girls were kind and patient and it was nice to have them fussing over us. Most of us enjoyed our lessons, and at the end, if we stayed calm and behaved nicely, we got a treat. A lovely sweet treat which crunched in our teeth and tasted strongly of mint. Soon, Joe and me were waiting at the gate for our lessons. We didn't mind the brush or the hoof pick or the halter and tried hard to learn what we needed to do.

The girls already knew that Joe and me were best friends, so sometimes they let us into the pen together. Sometimes Joe was led in front, and me behind, and sometimes the other way round. Soon we were walking and trotting round the pen alongside the girls at our head. Most days it was fun. And at the end we got our treat.

Time went by, our days spent happily enough, but as the nights grew longer and the wind began to blow cold, life changed again.

For most of the yearlings it was time to start training. All of us were taken back on the lorry to the stables and given our own space which became our home for most of the day. Although there was hay to eat and straw under our feet, being in the same small space each day and only being allowed out to do our work made the freedom of the pasture seem like a distant memory. How we longed to fun free again! But at least we still had our friends, even if we could only speak to them across the yard or in the next stable.

The routine was the same each day. Small groups walked in the big round machine first, then in pairs they were taken to the sand pen, saddled up, and the smallest of the girls sat on their backs, for just a short time, and then longer. As time went on, they were ridden outside with some older horses next to them. Although I was not in training like the others, Joe would tell me where he had been when he got back from his work. Usually it was up to the long hill on the East of the farm, and there they would be allowed to gallop until the hill became steep and they ran out of breath and had to slow down. Then they would walk back together in a long line, breathing heavily and shaking their heads in the cold morning air.

One morning there was more activity on the yard than usual. Several shiny cars arrived and the extra people got out and went into the farmhouse. When they came out, the horses were already on their way to the gallops and the people followed on in the pickup, with John. There they sat watching the horses gallop by, one with binoculars, following them closely. After all the horses had been put away in their boxes the people came to look around the yard. Several of them stopped at Joe's stall which was next to mine and patted his neck, saying how well he had done. Grace walked around her box as it always took her longer to settle after work. She loved to run, and being inside had made her stressed and anxious. I watched everything with my head over the half door.

"Well thank you John, it's been a pleasure, as always. We'll be in touch, but at the moment it looks like we'll take the chestnut and the grey filly, and the dark bay in the end stable" said one of the men.

"Right," John replied, we'll get the papers sorted in time for next week and see you then."

They all shook hands and went back to their shiny cars and drove away. Although I did not understand their words, I had a bad feeling in my stomach about it all.

And then it happened. The next week the big horse box was brought around to our yard and three horses were taken away. One of them was Joe. I ran around my stable whinnying, calling for the best friend I had in all the world. Joe called back from the inside of the horse box, but it was no use and I watched as the ramp was raised and locked shut and the horse box slowly disappeared from view.

***

For the first time I can remember, life did not seem worth living. The ache in my heart from losing Joe was more than I could bear. Seeing his long brown face over the stable door every morning gave me hope. Every day now I looked across to his stable, and every morning I remembered that he was no longer there. The girls tried to make me feel better, but it wasn't the same. I tried to concentrate on my lessons, but it was no fun any more. Finally, Fiona could stand it no longer.

"John, why did you let Joe go?" she said as they walked across the yard and took off their boots at the farmhouse door. "I've been talking to Maureen and Sophie. They think Malé is pining for him, and he was coming along so well."

"He'll get over it" John replied.

"I don't want him getting over it. Can't we ask Banningtons if we can have Joe back? We've plenty of horses, he didn't need to take that one!"

"He liked Joe, and he has a great pedigree. He'll do well at Banningtons. And that's got to be good for us in the long run."

"I know but.....John, please. Let me just ask how he's getting on and take it from there?"

John shook his head as he hung his flat cap on the peg by the door. Fiona smiled and kissed his cheek as they went through the white farmhouse door.

"Looks like Joe might be coming back, young man," Sophie whispered as she gave me my hay.

"I'll bet you a fiver he does" Maureen said, as she lifted the dirty straw into the wheelbarrow.

"Yep," said Sophie, "Fiona always gets her way in the end."

And it was only a few days before Joe was back, just like he'd never been away.

The show

As soon as Joe got back, he was put into the stable next to me so we could talk to each other through the metal bars between the stalls. It wasn't like being out in the fields together, but it would have to do, and I didn't care as long as Joe was by my side again.

It was so good to get out of the stable together each day with the girls to do our work. Just the other side of the farmhouse, away from the yard, there was a small field, but it had no grass, just lots of tiny grey pieces on the ground, with a wooden fence all around it and a hedge which we could just see over if we stretched out necks. It was here we were taken to practice all the things we needed to do to please the humans. I am not sure why we did some things, or why the humans should be so pleased with us for doing them, but I never forgot my mother's words when she told me that life would be easier if I did.

First, we would be allowed to run around for a few minutes, just the get the tickle out of our feet, as the girls said, then we would have the lead rope attached to our halters and start today's lesson. By now, both Joe and I could walk and trot next to the girl at our head, and slow down and stop when they asked. We stood still to have a saddle put on, and learnt not to be afraid of the long thin whip as we were touched all over with it. Next came the bit. This is a piece of metal with a joint in the middle which goes in our mouths, and a ring either side that the leap rope is attached to. You have to be careful of this piece of metal, as if you

41

pull away sharply, it jabs you in the tongue and mouth and it can hurt. Then, we were shown lots of scary objects, like plastic bags which rustle in the breeze, bright orange cones with flags sticking out of the top, and a huge piece of plastic that we had to walk over. Joe went first. He is always very calm when new things happen. I waited until he was safely over it before I followed him. We both got a sweet mint for that, so it wasn't so bad.

But best of all was when we got to jump. Jumps are quite simple. They are a long pole held off the ground by a wooden frame either side. They are painted in bright colours, but Joe and me had seen them many times before and had stepped over the poles plenty of times with the girls. Then, one day, the rope was removed from my halter and I was asked to canter around the field along the fence. Joe was held in the middle, to watch for a while. When I turned the second corner at the shorter side, I saw the jump in front of me. It was bigger than the ones before, a little too big to step over and I was now cantering quite fast. There was only one thing for it – up and over I went, clearing the jump by at least the height of my bucket. For some reason it made me so happy I tossed my head and bucked for the sheer joy of it after I landed safely the other side.

Then it was Joe's turn. I wanted to run with him, but Sophie, who stood at my head said no, I should wait, and she held tightly onto the rope, even when I shook my head impatiently. I know that Joe loved to gallop, but it seems we were much the same when it came to jumping too. He also cleared the little jump with inches to spare. The girls then made it higher and we went again. By now it was about as high as our knees. Again, Joe and me both cleared it with ease and tossed our heads.

The girls smiled and patted our necks.

"Shall we put it up again?" Sophie said. "Just to see what they can do?"

"Better not," Maureen replied, "Fiona will have our guts for garters if she catches us jumping her precious Malé."

"Well that's a bit rubbish," Sophie answered, "they both looked like they were having a whale of a time to me. Not just Malé." And they both smiled.

We were walked around quietly to help us calm down before going back to our stables.

Then came the day when we were joined in our work by Fiona herself. We did all the usual things, which by now Joe and me were very good at. Fiona watched while we trotted up and down in front of her. She watched carefully and then set out some poles for us to walk over. When we did that without touching one she said "I think it's time we saw them jumping, don't you?" The girls exchanged glances and the Sophie handed my rope to Fiona while she set up a tiny jump in the usual place along the long side of the field.

"Let Joe do it first," Fiona said, and Joe was unclipped from the rope and with a tap of the whip on Maureen's boot, he cantered off happily and cleared the jump so easily I was sure Fiona would guess we'd

43

done it all before. Then it was my turn. I decided I would make the most of having an audience and made a huge leap over the pole without breaking stride at all. Fiona laughed and clapped. Smiling, she turned to the girls as they brought us to stand in front of her.

"Amazing," she said, "they're obviously naturals. It's as if they've done it all before!"

"Well, he's a chip off the old block, for sure," Maureen said, stroking my face. Sophie hid her smiling face behind Joe's neck.

"Better get them cool and back in the stable. We don't want them getting cold," Fiona replied. "Thank you both. They're more than ready for the show," and she turned and let herself out of the field.

"I think we got away with that one!" Sophie said.

"Yep. I think we did. Just," replied her friend.

***

One morning, a few days after Fiona came to watch us working, we had an early start to the day. The girls arrived before it was properly light carrying their boxes of brushes and bottles of dark oily stuff to put on our hooves and tiny bands for our manes. After our food, we were brushed and combed until our coats shone and our manes and tails were smooth, then each bit of mane was made into a plait, then rolled up tightly and secured with one of the tiny bands. Then, each hoof was cleaned out with the metal hoof pick, wiped clean with a small towel and oil was brushed onto each hoof inside and out. After that, we had our lightest rugs put on and were led out to the big yard where the horse box was waiting, the back ramp down all ready for us to walk straight on. Joe and me were tied up inside next to each other and settled down to eat our hay. One of the girls got into the driver's seat and the other went to the farmhouse to tell Fiona we were ready to leave. The girl then climbed up beside her friend, and Fiona got into her own car. The horse box started up and we swayed as it pulled through the electric gates out onto the tarmac road.

Joe and me were used to travelling in the horse box, so we were not afraid. The sides were padded in case we bumped our haunches on them, and we soon learnt to balance and eat at the same time. Soon we were surrounded by traffic and the smell filled our nostrils so we snorted and shook our heads, but sometimes, through the open window, we also smelt grass and trees and a fresh wind.

Soon the horse box ride became bumpy as we drove slowly across an enormous grass field, and came to a stop. I was impatient to see where we were. I hoped it was a field where Joe and me could run free again, as we used to when we were younger, and I stretched my neck towards the window to see. But as the door opened I could see that this was not a field to gallop about in. It was full of people, horse-boxes, cars, large white tents, as far as we could see. In one part, which was fenced off with white ropes, there were some large jumps, bigger than Joe and me had ever seen. We were led from the box, taking our time down the steep ramp and set off for a walk, following the girls, as we had been taught.

There was noise and movement everywhere we looked, in every direction there were horses and people and vehicles, the air seemed to be buzzing with all the activity. There was a light breeze so it was cool despite a warm Spring sun. I began to prance with the excitement of it all, shaking my head and snorting. Joe walked calmly beside Maureen.

"Hey, calm down Malé, you'll be standing on someone's toes!"

"It's his first show, he's bound to be a bit wound up. Give him a break!"

"As long as it's not my toes that get a break."

"He'll soon settle. Let's take them over to the collecting ring, we have to meet Fiona there, and it might be quieter."

The girls were right, the collecting ring was much quieter, being well away from the main part of the show at the bottom of the long slope. The man at the rope gate checked his paperwork and let us through. There were a few other young horses there looking just like us with plaits in their manes and shiny coats. We ate a little grass and strolled around some more and then Fiona waved at us from behind the ropes. She was dressed very smartly, not in her usual jeans and sweatshirt, with a tweed hat, not the usual wooly one.

"How long do we have?" Fiona asked the girls.

"Plenty of time – about twenty minutes. Your class is in ring four, second from the top, on the left."

"Thank you" Fiona answered. "And how is my beautiful boy today?" She stroked my neck with her gloved hand. I turned to smell her pockets in case she had a sweet for us, but I couldn't smell anything. She smiled and suddenly looked sad. The girls glanced at each other. Both of them remembered my mother as they had cared for her when she had her previous foals, and both were around on that dreadful day when she passed.

Suddenly brisk, Fiona said "Ok. Well, I'll see you up there. They both look very nice, thank you. I think there might be some rosettes to take home," and she ducked under the rope and went back to her car.

The girls fiddled with our plaits and wiped some dust from our coats with a damp cloth and Maureen took off her blue overalls to reveal her smart clothes underneath, then we set off back up the field to the ring. The noise again filled our ears and I just could not stand still. We walked up and down some more until it was time to go into the ring. Fiona took my lead rope and gently rubbed my neck. It seemed so very important to her that I was here today, and although I did not really understand why, I tried my best to concentrate. All we had to do was walk around in a big circle, a bit like we did in the schooling field at home, but with lots more horses we had never met before, all with their human at their heads. Then we had to stand in a long line, and each of us trotted in front of the two people in the middle, taking our turn. I was quite glad for the chance to pick up some speed, and happily ran alongside Fiona, lifting my slender legs up high. Although she was breathing quite hard when we turned, and even harder when we finished and returned to the line, she smiled and nodded at the men in charge and they smiled back, so I hoped I had done well. Next in line was Joe, with Maureen in her smart clothes. I think Joe looked beautiful with his shiny red coat and both his legs white below his knees flashing past as he trotted by.

It seemed like a very long time for us all to be seen, but Fiona kept speaking to me and stroking my nose and helping me to stay still. At last, the men in charge finished their discussions and asked three of us to step forward from the long line. First Joe, then me, and then a bay filly with legs nearly as long as mine. The men handed out rosettes with ribbons which fluttered in the breeze. Mine was blue, Joe's was red, and the bay filly's, yellow. We all walked round with the rosettes attached to our bridles, but when I shook my head to get rid of it, Fiona laughed, and put it in her pocket. Joe tried to eat his, but I don't expect it tasted very nice as he soon spat it out.

"You'll have to get used to winning rosettes young man!" came a voice from the sidelines. It was John, who had been watching from the other side of the ropes.

"Didn't he do well!" Fiona called. "First time out and took second place."

"And who would have thought Joe would be such a star. First in this turnout is quite something" John replied as he fell in step with us.

"I told you it was better for him to be here with us."

"Maybe!" John smiled at her. "We'll see how he gets on when the real work starts."

"He'll be fine, I'm sure," Fiona said, "with that pedigree and such a calm nature. He's going to be a winner too."

"Even better if he can teach Malé not to fidget."

Fiona handed my lead rope to Sophie and took the blue rosette from her pocket.

"Here, this is as much yours as mine. Thanks for getting him ready. I know you've both worked hard with these two."

"Just doing our job. But thank you. We'll hang the rosettes in the horsebox where everyone can see them," Sophie replied.

"And let's hope there'll be plenty more to come," Fiona smiled.

Fiona took her hat from her head and fanned her face as she caught up with John on his way towards the tents.

Joe changes career

When Joe first came home he still had to go out onto the gallops every day except Sunday, with the other young horses in training. But one day, all that was to change.

Whilst Joe was out on the gallops I tried to be as calm as possible. After all, he would soon be back in the stable next to me. I stretched my neck as far out of the half door as I could, as soon as I heard the horses feet on the track, or saw a brightly coloured blanket waving in the wind as the line of horses made their way back to the yard, each with their jockey perched on top.

But one day, Joe came back before the other horses with only Breeze with him. I wasn't expecting him so early but I was very glad to see him and whinnied a happy greeting as the gate was opened and Joe strolled through.

Maureen came out of the end stable with the wheelbarrow, bolting the door behind her.

"What's happened?" she called to Craig, the jockey who usually rode Joe. She glanced up the track to see where the other horses were.

Craig swung his right leg over Joe's back and dropped neatly to the floor.

"Young Joe has been having us on, Maureen," he said. "All this time we thought he was a racehorse. Turns out he's really a showjumper all along." Craig unbuckled Joe's girth and pulled the saddle and blanket over Joe's back and placed it over the nearest

51

stable door. He took off his hat and rubbed his forehead. Sophie appeared from the little room at the end of the yard with some steaming mugs of tea.

Craig took one and thanked Sophie and drank half of it down before he told the story.

"Well, we were on the way to the gallops, about half way along the track, just before Sellars Wood."

"Up by the bridle path?" Sophie interrupted, as she sipped her tea.

"Yes, just past there," Craig replied. "Joe and me were almost at the front, like normal, and all of a sudden, a couple of horses came cantering down the hill from the moor."

"Were they from the riding school?" Maureen asked.

"I think so," Craig replied.

"They're not supposed to do that. John's asked them at least a dozen times to go a bit steady down that hill," Maureen said, as she put Joe back into the stable next to me.

"I know, but today it all went a bit pear shaped. We were about at the front when the horses came cantering down, and Joe thought it might be fun to join them" Craig explained.

"Ooh Joe, you little pest!" said Maureen patting his neck.

"So he swung round on his hind legs and went off after them. But that's where the bridle path narrows off so…"

"So?"

"So Joe went right on up and over the fence into the field. He nearly had me off, I can tell you."

"The fence into the riding school field? But that's higher than my waist!"

"It's higher than my neck!"

"Yes, but that's cos you're a jockey."

"What? Joe just jumped right over the fence?"

"Yep. I let him canter on a bit and brought him round in a circle back to the rest, but the head lad said it wasn't safe for him to jump back so I'd have to walk him back to the riding school and head back along the road. He sent Charlotte on Breeze to walk with us so he wasn't stressing on his own."

"Joe never stresses, bless him," Maureen said. "Look out, here comes the boss." She nodded towards the house, where Fiona was getting her boots on at the door. Sophie got her broom and started sweeping, and Craig picked up the saddle and headed towards the tack room. Maureen gathered the mugs and met Fiona as she entered the yard.

She was smiling, as she stopped to stroke my face, then went straight over to Joe, who had been drinking from the bucket in his stable and water dripped from his muzzle as he hung his head over the half door and greeted Fiona.

"Well, my red friend, what have you been up to then?" she asked him as she patted his shiny neck. Craig joined her and told her the story of what had happened.

"Yes, John rang through and told me. Wasn't Joe marvelous! Who'd have thought it. Another show-jumper in the making!"

Maureen and Sophie exchanged puzzled glances across the yard as they busied themselves with their chores.

"How did he feel?" Fiona asked Craig. Craig relaxed as he realized he wasn't in trouble.

"Well" said Craig, getting into his stride, "At first I thought Joe would just ignore the other horses, being the laid back creature that he is, but when they swung past him, he wasn't being left behind. No way, he was after them and caught up in two strides. And then, I thought he might think better of it and slow down, with the fence being in the way and all, but he didn't and we were over it before I knew what was happening. And I'm sure there was plenty more in the engine than that, the way he went over."

"Amazing!" Fiona exclaimed. "He'll definitely have to come out of training now. We can't have a potential talent like that wasted. He'll have to join Malé on the show circuit until they're old enough to start their jumping education."

"Craig! What the hell happened with that horse?" It was John who had pulled up in the landrover and was striding across the yard to Joe's stable.

"Well, Sir," Craig began, a little nervously, but Fiona interrupted.

"Oh John, keep your hair on. Joe was just showing us his career preferences. He can join Malé and they can both be show jumpers."

"Fiona, in case you've forgotten, we breed racehorses. You know, to race! The fastest gets the prize, that thing...."

"Well, we can always diversify," she suggested, helpfully.

"I'm a racehorse trainer. I don't bloody want to diversify. You've got your potential showjumper with Malé, against my better judgement, with his breeding. He could have been the next Shergar!"

"Hmm... yes, and look what happened to him" Fiona answered.

Just then, the first horses arrived back from the gallops, and moments later, the yard was full of potential racehorses back from their work, jockeys jumped down, discussing how the day's work had gone. Maureen and Sophie appeared from the tack room to take them from their jockeys and get them untacked and settled back in their stables.

Fiona smiled at John, her head on one side in her most endearing way.

"Gaahhhhhh!!!" said John. "I give in!" and he went back to the farmhouse with his cap in his hand and slammed the door behind him. Joe, sensing he was the centre of attention at least for a short while, tossed his head up and down, curling his lip and showing his big yellow teeth, making everyone smile.

A working horse

Life was pleasant enough as the months passed. Joe and me grew broader and stronger, although of course, our legs did not get any longer, as every foal is born with their lower legs fully grown.

Since Joe was no longer in training as a racehorse, we got to spend much more time together, sometimes even out in the fields with two older geldings whose owners kept them on when they retired and were quite happy for them to spend their days quietly away from the hustle and bustle of the racecourse. They didn't mind Joe and me sharing their field, as long as we didn't pester them too much.

In our fourth year, after a long cold winter, the Spring came late and tiny petals from blossom in the hedgerows swirled onto our yard, carried by the fresh wind. We sniffed the air over our stable doors, smelling the new grass, flowers and damp earth. Life was returning to the earth after its long sleep.

Every day we were allowed out of our stables while they were cleaned, with our blue rugs firmly strapped around our bodies. Joe and me were let out together in the small field by the yard to run around while the younger horses in training went up to the gallops as soon as it was light. After a while, we were brought back in for our morning feed, then our coats were brushed and our feet cleaned out ready for our day's work.

More muscle and stronger bones meant that our training took up more of our time, and being out in the pasture like when we were young now became a treat we did not experience as often as we would have liked. Now our energy was diverted into our work and there didn't seem to be time for very much else.

There was a lot to get used to. Maureen and Sophie continued to show us what to do. There was lots of stepping over poles, learning how to bend around corners, how to slow down when we were asked, going faster or slower or changing gait when we were told. Soon we were ready to be ridden and it was usually Sophie as she was the lightest, with Maureen leading the way as we walked and trotted round the field. Since Joe had already been ridden when he was a racehorse in training, he seemed to learn faster than me. I found it strange to have a human on my back. The extra weight meant it wasn't so easy to balance and it was quite tiring. Seeing someone on my back out of the corner of my eye reminded me that long ago, horses were food for lots of wild animals and to stay safe it was best to run as fast as you could back to the herd until you were amongst your family again. But with the bit in our mouths in a small field we could not run very far and there was no herd to hide amongst.

Joe tried to help me. "There are no tigers, Malé," he would say, "only the humans. And I am close by," and I would listen to his words and try to worry less.

One day when we were riding out on the roads near to the yard we came across an enormous noisy vehicle with bright red claws on the front. It rattled and banged as its tyres rumbled along, and it came so close I was afraid. I tried to run, but the bit pulled hard on the sides of my mouth and I reared up on my hind legs striking out with my front hooves. Joe tried to run to my side but the vehicle was in the way and it wasn't until it had rattled passed that he could stand beside me as I stood shaking and snorting in fear. The vehicle made its way up the road. Sophie was still on my back and she leaned forward to pat my neck while Maureen shouted at the driver of the vehicle, though he was long gone and could not hear her.

"Bloody idiot tractor drivers," she said, "You OK Soph?"

"Yeah, I'm OK. Bit close for comfort though." Sophie took a deep breath and patted my neck reassuringly. "Phew!"

"Let's get these two back and let John know, he'll have words for that driver for sure."

So we went back to the yard at a brisk trot so that by the time we reached the big wooden gates I was tired and glad to be safely back again where everything was familiar and quiet and everyone tried hard to keep us safe.

Fiona came out of the farmhouse as Sophie dismounted and led me through the gates.

"That was a brisk trot girls, everything OK?" she said. We are not allowed to trot on the roads like that normally, as Fiona says it is too hard on our legs and we should walk steadily to build up our bones slowly and not damage our tendons.

"Yes, sorry about that. We had a brush with a racing tractor. Some idiot got too close just as we'd turned onto the road from the bridlepath and Malé stood on his hindlegs in protest."

"Oh," said Fiona, "are you all alright? No falls or anything?"

"No, I stayed on, just about!" Sophie answered.

"Nice work! No harm done then?"

"No, but it might have set Malé back a bit on the roads. I don't understand it, the locals all know the horses turn onto the road there and they're usually sensible enough to give us a bit of room." Maureen handed Joe to Sophie and she took us both back to our stables while she spoke to Fiona about it.

"You're right, they normally take a bit more care going through the village. I think I heard John on the phone to William's when he was ordering the hay. Apparently they've lost Fred, their old tractor driver recently, gone to live with his daughter, Salisbury way I think, and it was a bit quick, so they've had to get a contractor in. I'll ask him when I get back in and go and have a word on my way to the Post Office later."

"That would be a help. It was pretty scary. Sophie did well to stay on. Malé was pretty spooked."

"Yes, that's good. That none of you were hurt. It could have been a disaster." A shadow seemed to cross Fiona's face as she looked towards the stables where her beloved Malé's face looked out.

"We're all OK, that's the main thing," Maureen said quickly, "and we'll make sure Malé gets more road work once he's got over the shock. Build it up gradually again. Keep Joe with him."

Fiona's face softened as she heard Joe and me whinny when Sophie came out of the feed room with our buckets. She almost smiled.

"Yes. Thank you. And thank Sophie too, for me."

Maureen nodded and smiled as she made her way across the yard to start filling hay nets for the night.

"Did we get away with that one then?" Sophie asked as she dropped another armful of nets at Maureen's feet.

"Yeah, course. You know how she worries. She said to thank you."

"Me? What for?"

"For not falling off and needing an ambulance. And for getting Marls back in one piece. I dunno, but that tractor driver might seriously regret his choice of career later on."

"Why? Does she know who it is?"

"She said it was Williams's new contractor. Going over there for a word later."

"Holy Shit," said Sophie. "He's so dead."

"Totally," Maureen agreed.

Up and away

"John! It's arrived. It's here!" Fiona lifted her laptop up towards John as he came down the farmhouse stairs to the kitchen.

"What's here? Have Banningtons paid their bill on time for once?"

"No. You know they always pay when they've sent the cattle to market and not a second before. No, it's the district show schedule."

"Oh, that local one. Beer tents and flower arranging and suchlike."

"Yes, the first one of the season. Time to get Malé and Joe spruced up and show the world how good they are."

"About time they proved themselves. Might even earn their keep one day."

"I doubt it!" Fiona answered. "well, not until Malé has some eventing points at least."

"And is that part of the plan? To take him eventing this season?"

"Oh definitely," she replied. "We'll see how he goes in a small local show, and next month he can go to something at county level, and then…"

"And then he'll be knackered," John interrupted, dodging the damp tea towel Fiona hurled in his direction on his way out to the yard, stopping only to grab his cap from the peg by the door. Fiona tutted, then turned her attention back to the laptop to start filling in her entry form.

Now that we were on our way to becoming event horses, it was time for Fiona to take over some of our ridden sessions. Sophie still rode Joe, as she was younger and needed the experience, but I was ridden by Fiona in the arena. First, she would watch us warm up, walking and trotting and then we had a rest while Fiona discussed with the girls what we would spend the session doing. We might do circles, or changes of pace, or practicing stopping calmly, or bending, even going backwards. Most times we did some work with poles, but Fiona left these till the end, as I tended to get excited in anticipation of jumping practice. Maureen and Sophie would lay out the poles in a grid, or in a long line, and Joe and me had to walk or trot or canter carefully over them. At the end we often did some small jumps, no taller than our knees, and we had to concentrate and balance ourselves and make sure our feet were in the right place ready for when the next one came up.

One day we just had two jumps along the long sides of the arena, and these were higher than we had done before. We had to practice cantering past them steadily first and then it was time to jump them both. Fiona's hands on the reins guided me on the right line, and for a brief second, I felt a little daunted, but Fiona sat quietly in the saddle and I tucked up my front feet and pushed off hard to clear the jump by a long way. Fiona wasn't expecting such a big effort, and she lost a stirrup on landing, and I picked up speed, a little worried by the metal catching my side, but she soon regained it and we went over the second one with a smaller leap.

"Well sat!" called Maureen, from the end of the arena where she was sitting on the mounting block. Fiona slowed me down and we halted right next to her on our next round.

"That's some jump he's got there! Are you OK?"

"Yes, just about." Fiona was smiling as she jumped to the ground and patted my neck. "Just like his mother. Meg was just the same. She loved her jumping too."

Then it was Joe's turn, and he cleared both the jumps with ease and came to a halt beside us. He turned to nip my neck playfully and I stepped sideways then stretched my neck to nip him back.

"Hey you two, that's enough fun for one day. Let's get you cooled off and your rugs back on. And then it's lunch time for you both." Fiona handed my reins to Maureen and she and Sophie loosened our girths and walked us around the arena, tidying up the poles and stands as they went.

"Maureen, can you make sure Malé gets some of that new supplement this week? And Joe of course. They're going to need it with their schedule this season," Fiona said.

"Yes, you mean the joint one? In the blue tub?" Maureen answered.

"That's the one. Just a teaspoon to start with then…. Oh, you know what to do. Sorry. Of course you do. I'll go and sort out some paperwork or something" and she walked away, pulling off her gloves and putting them in her hard hat.

As we walked back to the yard I said to Joe: "That was fun. I like jumping." And Joe said "Yes, it's not as much fun as running free in the field, like we used to, but it will have to do."

Career horses

"Major! Quit banging about! I'm going as quick as I can." Maria jumped down from the horse box cab and hurried to the rear door. Reaching up to undo the top bolts, her father joined her and undid the other side so the big wide door could swing down and rest on the ground. Major tossed his head and stamped, making the whole box sway and rattle. Maria's brother strolled past.

"I'm going to find the beer tent," he said.

"Thanks for all your help," Maria shouted as he walked away. "Not," she added bitterly.

"Never mind him, he'd only be in the way. Stand back and I'll get this horse off for you before he wrecks the joint." Maria stepped to the side of the ramp with folded arms, as her dad clipped the longer rope to Major's headcollar, undid the shorter one which was still tied to the ring in the side of the box and undid the partition. Major knew it was time to be let out and shook his head and danced about impatiently. Maria's dad held the lead rope and pushed the partition clear as Major swung round to face the open door. Despite his impatience the rope held him firm and he stretched out his neck to balance as he went down the ramp where Maria took him and walked briskly between the rows of horse boxes to settle him down as he tossed his head, pranced and snorted. A small patch of sweat appeared on his neck and Maria sighed irritably.

"Major, mate, if you'd just calm down you wouldn't get hot and sweat like that. Do me a favour and save it for later, eh?"

Major had been to many shows, and he soon remembered that there was nothing to fear and when they returned to their own horse box he stood quietly in the shade pulling wisps of hay from the haynet, while Maria took off his rugs and travelling boots. Her father opened the smaller side door and started getting out the saddle and bridle and other bits of tack which Major wore.

"Hey, guess who I just saw?" Maria's brother reappeared with a burger in one hand and a can of Pepsi in the other.

"I dunno. The tooth fairy?" Maria answered as she continued to brush Major's sturdy wide back.

"Who?" their father answered, keen to avoid yet another argument between his son and daughter.

"Fiona Weston!" He smiled triumphantly as he munched another mouthful of burger.

"What?" Maria shouted, dropping the brush she was holding, making Major take a step away from her.

"What are Weston's doing here? I thought they had racehorses," their father answered.

"Well, unless they took the wrong turning at Cottam I'd say they were competing. No point coming here in that huge horsebox with two horses to stand around looking at flowers."

"Two horses?" Maria picked up the brush, threw it in the box with the others and came round to fetch the saddle. "Great stuff. That means we might get third place at best. Marvellous."

"Why's that then? Isn't it a bit early to say? You haven't even fallen off yours yet" said her brother, as he crammed the last of his burger into his mouth.

"You know why, Damian, Fiona has the pick of all the horses on the yard that her husband just happens to breed every year, a whole farm to ride on… a whole set of show jumps…. People to do the hard work for her. Nobody else stands a chance when she turns up. It's just not fair."

"Come on now," her father interrupted, "no point thinking like that. You've worked hard too, and even if you don't have a fancy set of show jumps Major's a good horse and he'll try his best for you."

Maria gazed at Major, looking thoughtful.

"I know Dad. I love the jumps you made us. We'll just have to do our best and that will have to be good enough."

"That's the spirit. Now come on and get tacked up. You've got half an hour till you're on."

***

Although this was not the first time at a show, since Joe and I had been to a few by this time, it was my first time as a show jumper. We had practiced so much recently I felt confident I would be able to clear all the jumps and make Fiona and the girls proud. Joe, of course, was by my side most of the time, ridden by Sophie who looked very different in her white jodhpurs and dark jacket. Her feet were in shiny black boots, not the old green wellington boots she normally wears on the yard. Fiona joined us as we walked from the horse box to the collecting ring to warm up.

"Everything OK girls?" Fiona said as she fell in step in between Joe and me.

"Yes, everything's been fine," Maureen answered, "They've both travelled really well and Malé doesn't seem too hyper. We've walked them about and they both seem good."

"Yes, they're looking very well," Fiona said, "Sophie, are you nervous? Try to relax. We're just here for the experience – to see how they go."

Sophie smiled nervously and fiddled with Joe's girth.

"I've not jumped in the ring since I was twelve," she said.

"It's just like riding a bike," said Fiona, "you never forget." They both mounted and we walked across the collecting ring. Maureen checked my girth and boots and then we had a canter and jumped the single pole jump set up in the middle from both directions.

Although I felt a little nervous, Fiona sat quietly and Joe stayed by my side. There were so many horses and people and so much to see. Soon it was Joe's turn to do his round and Maureen came to join us as we watched from the other side of the ropes. Sophie kept Joe moving steadily and guided him round the course right to the centre of each jump. He had no trouble at all until it came to the two jumps along the long side, quite close together. Joe was going a little too fast by this time and hit the second one with his hind leg and the pole fell. The people around the outside 'oohed' as the pole clattered onto the grass but they still clapped as Joe left the ring.

"Four faults for Josie's Bar of Gold, ridden by Sophie Jones. A promising combination, I'm sure you'll agree," said the announcer and Joe came back to join us.

"Bad luck at the combination," Maureen said.

"My fault. He was coming a bit too fast and dropped a hind leg on landing," Sophie answered, jumping down from Joe's back and running the stirrups up the leathers.

"And the next to jump, number eighteen, Fiona Weston with her newest entry Meg's Finalé, by the well-known stallion Meadow Valley Dancer," came the announcer's voice. It was our turn at last.

We trotted into the ring and down the long side, then Fiona asked me to canter, in the steady rhythmic way we had been practicing all year. She took me along the short side of the arena and then right past the combination where Joe had knocked one down, where it was all set up properly again. Then we turned towards the middle and the first of eight jumps. I tucked my feet up carefully and pushed off with my hind legs and we were over. Back to the steady canter ready for the left hand turn, number two safely cleared. Then we picked up a bit of speed as the next jump was a broader spread and I stretched out over it as Fiona crouched in the saddle with her hands well forward. Then back to the steady canter, change legs for the right hand bend. Number five was the biggest yet, but I tucked my feet up carefully and we were over. Then the combination. Fiona sat quietly and we kept our speed down and my stride was just the right length and both jumps stayed up. We hadn't touched either of them! Just a steady turn to the last and it was over. Fiona patted my neck as we slowed to a trot and left the ring.

"And a clear round for Fiona Weston and Meg's Finalé. A good steady round for this young horse's first outing," the announcer said.

"Brilliant!" said Maureen, as we joined her and Joe and Sophie back in the collecting ring.

"Wasn't he marvellous?" Fiona said, breathing hard as she jumped down and handed the reins to Maureen. She patted my neck again and Joe and me each got a sweet.

"You were marvellous too, Mister Joe!" Fiona said, "but no prizes for you today. I'll go and get a drink and meet you back here for the jump off. OK?"

Maureen nodded, smiling as she threw a light rug over my hind quarters.

"Cheer up," Maureen said to Sophie. "There'll be other shows you know."

"I know," Sophie answered, "but I feel as if I've let Joe down."

"I might be wrong, but he doesn't look too upset to me. In fact, I'd say he didn't care one little bit." Joe was munching on the grass now his bridle was off and his lightest rug had been put on while he cooled down.

Sophie looked thoughtful. "Do you think they enjoy it?" she said.

"I dunno really," Maureen answered. "They enjoy getting the best of everything and being pampered all the time I expect. They eat better than we do."

Sophie smiled at last. "Food. I'm hungry. What do you want from the van?"

"I thought you'd never ask," Maureen answered. "I'll have a hot dog and a can please. But be quick, it's the jump off in about ten minutes."

Sophie hurried away, leaving Maureen with Joe and me walking slowly around until Fiona came to take me back into the ring for the jump off. There were only four horses to go, me, a big black and white horse who looked a bit like my mother, and a grey with a long flowing mane and tail and a bay. The black and white horse went in first while we watched.

"Get in there Major!" said a voice from the sideline. His rider smiled, then they started cantering down to the far end past the new combination and back up to the start. The bell went and Major began his round. Though he was more heavily built that Joe or me, he was very light on his hooves and it seemed that he and his rider knew each other very well. They seemed to be in harmony all the time and Major wasn't phased by the brightly coloured jumps or the crowds, but kept his mind on his job and made it all look easy and before very long they had finished their round and the man at the ropes opened the entrance for him to come out of the ring.

"A clear round for Maria Marks and Major. No stranger to our show here in Belton, and very nice to see you both again," the announcer said.

Then it was our turn. Although I was beginning to feel a little tired after our busy day I settled into a canter ready for the first jump. It was bigger than the previous ones, so I had to concentrate hard to make sure my feet didn't touch the poles. Fiona guided me round and made sure I had plenty of room to take off and land safely. The combination looked quite big this time, and I hesitated for a tiny moment but Fiona squeezed my sides gently to let me know what to do and we flew over it. Turning to the last, a dog got loose and came running across the arena towards me. For a second I flicked my ear towards the dog, but it was too far away to be near my feet and I jumped this one as I had done the others. As we landed, my hind foot just touched the pole, but it didn't fall. It bounded around in the cups and stayed up. The crowd went 'oooh' again and then clapped as we left the ring.

"A close one there for number 18, but still clear with a time of forty-eight seconds and into second place behind Maria Marks and Major," said the announcer.

After this, we could relax and Joe and me were given our food and were tied up beside the horse box to eat some hay while we waited for the class to finish. The black and white horse passed us, being led by his owner, and Fiona smiled and waved to them both. Fiona left us with Maureen and Sophie to collect her rosette, and she came back with not one but two!

"What happened?" Maureen asked as Fiona waved the blue and yellow rosettes excitedly.

"It's Joe's," she said "the other rider in the jump off didn't go as his horse lost a shoe, so the next best round gets fourth place. It was our Joe, so they're both in the ribbons after all!"

She handed the yellow rosette to Sophie, who thanked her and smiled.

"See, the last rosette since you were twelve," Fiona said.

"Oh, I didn't win a rosette then," Sophie answered. "I fell off at the third when Penny dodged the jump and legged it back to the entrance and one of the judges caught her for me."

"Really?" Fiona said. "I fell off in a dressage test once."

"In a dressage test?" said Maureen, "How..?"

"Don't ask," said Fiona.

***

"So there you go girl, Major did you proud again!" Maria's dad put his arm around his daughter as she arrived back at the horse box with her red rosette. She was beaming and hugged her dad.

"Thanks Dad," she said. "we couldn't have done it without you, you know."

"I know," said her dad. "It's just good to see a smile on your face, love. And there'll be plenty more later in the season. It's only April yet."

"Can we get home now?" said Damion. "I'm starving." For once Maria said nothing. She hung the rosette in the horse box on the string. The first of the season.

As they rumbled across the grass towards the lane her dad said: "Hey, you'll never guess who I was stood next to while you were jumping."

"Who?" said Maria.

"John Weston. Fiona's chap. He was telling me about that black horse of theirs that came second. He was orphaned the day he was born, you know."

"Awww poor thing!" said Maria.

"Yes, his dam started bleeding and there was nothing they could do. He's hardly ever out of sight of the chestnut that had a pole down at the second to last. Best pals they are."

"It is a boy horse, the chestnut?" Damion asked.

"You mean a gelding?" Maria corrected.

"Yes," said her father.

"How do you know that? That it's a gelding." Damian wanted to know.

"John told me," his father replied. "It was going to be a racehorse, you know, he sells them on every year to different yards when they go into training. All get gelded at nine months."

"I can't believe you talked about horse's balls to a complete stranger, Dad," Damian replied.

"And the black one, that lost his mum, is that a gelding? The announcer said it was by Meadow Valley Dancer, that horse that won the Grand National." Maria asked.

"Oh no," her father replied. "That one's entire. Got a top career ahead of him, they hope."

"Did you discuss that one's balls as well then?" Damian asked.

"No, I didn't, as it happens," said their father.

"So how do you know it's still a stallion then?"

"I did what normal people do son, I bent down and had a look."

"Oh Dad!!!" Maria said, and burst out laughing.

Rabbits

Although we had lots of practicing to do, and this was nearly always in the arena, some days we would go out for a long ride off the farm, through the village, up to the woods where it was cool in the summer and sheltered from the wind and rain in the winter. There was a meadow where Joe and I sometimes had a gallop. I made sure Joe didn't get left behind, but today, Sophie and Maureen had been asked to give us both a test. Maureen had been given a stop watch and she was to time Joe and me galloping between two points on the map. The distance had been worked out by Fiona and marked on the map Maureen had in her pocket. We had on our lightest saddles and simplest bridle. We stopped at the beginning of the grassy track which ended in a gently rising slope.

"Right," Maureen announced, "This is it. Stage one of event training. The gallop."

"But without the jumps in the way," Sophie reminded her.

"I bloody well hope so, or you and me are both dead."

"Right," Sophie replied. "Who's going first? What did Fiona say?"

"Both at the same time. Get them up to their best gallop in a few strides, then keep them at a steady pace until we pass the oak tree. No racing."

"No racing? Seriously? She does remember who these two are, right?"

Maureen, laughed, but a little nervously I thought. She fiddled with the paper, zipping it carefully back into her inside pocket, and both girls checked their stirrups and Maureen held the stopwatch in her hand.

"You ready?"

"Nope," said Sophie.

"Three, two, one…GO!"

This came as a bit of a surprise to Joe and me, as we don't normally gallop about like racehorses, but both Sophie and Maureen urged us on and Joe remembered his racehorse training and was off in full gallop. Thinking I would not be allowed to follow him, I tossed my head and pranced until Joe was a few strides ahead and I was not happy being left behind. So I launched myself after his broad chestnut quarters expecting to be pulled back, but Maureen crouched low in the saddle with her hands forward along my neck and encouraged me to stretch out my neck and we soon caught up and then we galloped side by side, with the hedgerows flashing past and dust flying from our hooves behind. A family of rabbits scattered from the far end of the field, their white scuts bobbing as they dived into their burrows away from the sound of our hoofbeats thundering through the ground. A bird flew out of an overhanging tree, screeching in annoyance at being disturbed but we were gone in a flash.

"Aaaannnndddd woooooahhh!" said Maureen as we approached the slope and the galloping grew harder and we were breathing hard. She sat back down in the saddle and I flicked my right ear backwards as

I heard the stopwatch click. I was quite glad to slow down and when we reached the gate at the top Maureen and Sophie both dismounted smiling and laughing at the exhilaration of it all as Joe and me stood panting side by side, our necks shimmering in the sun from sweat.

"What was the time? How did we do?" Sophie asked, panting and ducking under Joe's head to get a look at the stop watch in Maureen's hands.

"I dunno. Wait." Maureen got the paper out and a pencil. "Here, take Malé and I'll try and work it out." Sophie walked Joe and me to a patch of fresh green grass and we tucked in happily for a while, the sun drying the sweat from our necks.

Maureen had a look of concentration on her face, and she muttered to herself as she wrote down some figures, pressing numbers into her smartphone.

"So that's 68 seconds over 550 metres…. That's 8.5 metres per second…times by sixty… and that makes it 485 point 3 metres per minute." She wrote down the answers with the paper stretched across her hand.

"How did we do?" Sophie called over, impatient to know the results.

Maureen continued to mutter and write on the paper, juggling the stopwatch and the pencil and paper, checking what she had written.

"Just over 485 metres per minute. That's BE100 level" she said as she came over and took my reins from Sophie.

"Wow. That's good, right? I mean, what Fiona was expecting?"

"It's almost racehorse speed Soph. That's pretty much their season sorted. How's your cross country jumping?"

"Me? Apart from needing a change of underwear you mean?"

Maureen smiled. "That's gross. Yes! I mean you. Who else is going to ride Joe when Malé goes out?"

"Can't Fiona ride both of them? I'll just get him ready for her. I'm good at that."

"Not at the same time" Maureen answered. "Come on Soph, this is an opportunity of a lifetime. Top class racehorse turned eventer to bring on and you're worried about your underwear!"

"Why can't you do it? You're the more experienced rider." Sophie suggested.

"You know why. I'm too heavy. Too many doughnuts with my tea. There's less of you for Joe to carry."

"That's true. You do eat a lot of doughnuts. To keep the cold out in the winter you always say. And now it's summer."

"It is indeed. But I'm still not going to stop eating doughnuts."

"Why the heck not?"

"You'll not catch me going round those cross-country courses. Those fences don't fall down you know."

"You!!!!" Sophie punched her friend's arm playfully. They both laughed as they remounted and walked us back down the track to the village.

***

Once Joe and me were back in our stables with a meal and some hay to keep us busy Maureen and Sophie made their way across the yard to the farmhouse where Fiona was waiting.

"Come in!" she waved, as Sophie and Maureen stood on the whitewashed doorstep by the front porch. "Come in and tell me all about it! How did they go? How did Malé find it? I bet they wanted to race!" she asked, one question after another as she bustled about and poured fresh coffee from the machine by the kettle. The aroma of the freshly ground brew wafted across the room. She finally sat down, handing out mugs and pushing the sugar and cream across the table on a pretty blue tray.

Maureen spooned some sugar into her drink, stirring it briskly, then took a long drink, put down her mug and said 'Now that's a good cup of coffee!" Then she fiddled in her pocket for the stopwatch and the piece of paper she had written the numbers on. Smiling, she handed them over to Fiona.

"Oh!" said Fiona, studying the note carefully. "Well, that's... if I'm not much mistaken, that's quite a way up the scale." She turned in her chair and reached over to the dresser for a small, glossy booklet and flicked through it until she found the right page. "Here it is. I make that BE100 level. What do you think?" She passed the booklet to Maureen and Sophie peered over her shoulder.

"Yes, I make it that too. They're way above the novice level at that pace. 'Course, there weren't any jumps in the way, just a flat gallop."

"Yes, but it's good news they can keep up that pace and still only young. I'm really pleased with that. Thank you both." Fiona smiled as she looked at both girls. Then she looked at Sophie and asked: "So, how did Joe feel? Did you find it exciting?"

Sophie looked uncomfortable and then put down her mug and said "Yes, I did. Joe has a lovely gallop, and those two work so well together. But I am a bit... well, nervous about those fixed fences. You do hear some horror stories."

"Do you mean when Zara Philips fell off and had to be airlifted to hospital? She didn't even break her ankle, you know. But she's the queen's grand-daughter, so they pulled out all the stops. And it will be a slow build up you know. They won't be ready for anything but the first levels for at least a couple of years. I don't want to risk them getting injured or anything, not after...."

Sophie smiled. "I know it's an amazing opportunity Mrs Weston, please don't think I'm not grateful. But do you really think I'll be able to... you know... get up to scratch? I'm more of a dressage person really, so..."

"Events get won and lost on dressage tests, you know. And that's something Joe will excel at, he does look marvellous with those flashy white socks, really catches the judge's eye." Seeing Sophie looking less than ecstatic Fiona said "Well, how about we give it a go. Just for a season. We can take them over to Field Farm and start them off. They have some lovely little logs and things over there, just to get them going, and then you can see how it feels? I know you can do it, Sophie, you have an amazing rapport with a horse. Don't think I haven't noticed. All the horses are calm with you. Not just Joe. They feel safe, you see. We wouldn't have this yard running as smoothly as it does without you, not with twenty highly strung thoroughbreds around."

Sophie stared. "Oh. Do you think so? I hadn't really thought about it much."

"Well I have," Fiona said, "Let's give it a go, eh? Malé and Joe are practically joined at the hip. I can't imagine us getting far with either of them on their own. Just have a think about it. I'll get John to take us all over to the course next week. I'm sure you'll find it's fun once you're used to it."

"OK. I will. Think about it I mean," Sophie smiled and Maureen got up to leave.

"We'd best get on. Those stables won't muck themselves out," she said. "Thanks for the coffee." And they let themselves out of the farmhouse and made their way back to the yard.

Village Life

The door of the pub swung open and John Weston ducked his head to avoid the low beam as he stepped through the entrance to the Dog and Duck. Blinking in the darker interior he made his way to the bar.

"Usual John?" the landlord asked, wiping his hands on a small green towel and smiling as one of his best customers got out his wallet.

"Yes please," John replied. "Pint of your best brew, as always."

"Coming up!" said the landlord and lifted a clean pint glass from the rack, placed it carefully under the spout and pulled the brass handle so the amber liquid poured from the spout to just the right level with a small top of white foam.

"Here John!" called a voice from beside the open window, "Come and join us. We need to know who's going to win the 2.30 at Doncaster."

John turned and smiled. "Be with you in a minute," he replied and paid for his beer, separating the small coins and placing them in the charity box with a helicopter on the side.

"Very kind of you John," the landlord commented, "and a good choice of charity if I might say so. You never know when you might be in need of that air ambulance."

"Very true, Mac. Not for me really, but the jockeys might."

"I thought they didn't bother with hospitals when they fall off, them jockeys?" the landlord answered.

"Oh, they do, if we insist, but they always ignore what the doctors say."

They landlord chuckled and went back to polishing his glasses. John lifted his drink from the bar and took a sip as he turned and headed for his friends at the table.

"Now then John, what's going on in your little world? Can we rely on you to help us win a fortune this week, cos last week was no good at all!"

"Well, you know what it's like, you win some you lose some. It's a hard game, racing."

"Aye, it is. Wasn't that grey filly that won at Kempton one of yours? Won by more 'n a length."

"She wasn't, no," John replied. "But her dam was. Stressy mare, as I remember, but a cracking turn of speed if you could keep her mind on the job."

"Oh well, that's women for you!"

"I think they put her to Red Flag, Mitchell's stallion. Not a looker, but a steady type by all accounts. And that filly was the result."

They chatted for a while about the horses, farming, what the locals had been up to and then John's phone bleeped. He retrieved it from his pocket, checked the message and frowned.

"Oh what now?" He got up to leave, downing the last of his pint.

"Nothing bad I hope?" his friend enquired.

"Probably nothing. Horse off its food and showing signs of colic. Change of feed probably. I'd better go," and he strode off across the red tiled floor and the door banged shut behind him.

Reg looked up out of the window and watched as John's landrover turned out of the car park and sped off back to his yard, stones flying from the wheels.

"He's very dedicated, is John. All them people to look after them horses and he has to give up his evening pint cos one of 'em's got a bit of a belly ache," Mick observed.

Reg chuckled. "Oh, don't feel sorry for him. He'd have words to say if they called the vet out without him making the phone call. And his Missis don't let him get away with much. I'm surprised to see him, to be honest, on an ordinary Wednesday evening."

"Under the thumb is he, then?" Mick enquired.

"Oh I'll say so. But what you have to remember, Mick, is how it all came about. Him and that yard."

"Oh. I thought he'd inherited that land. Been in the family for generations?"

"No, no. Been in *her* family for generations. Fiona's, I mean."

"Ah. I see. So he picked the best filly out of the lot then?"

"After a fashion, Mick. You see, her great great grandfather, Sean Nichols, came over from Ireland with nothing but the clothes he was wearing and the cap in his hand. Fleeing one of them famines, they say. Well, he walked all the way from Liverpool docks, getting a few lifts here and there, sleeping in hedgerows and barns, ended up in this very pub and got chatting to the old boy that owned that farm who was in for his pint of ale and some good conversation. He was quite well off, having married the only daughter, who copped the lot when her folks passed on. But he had a passion for racehorses and no clue as to how to get into the game. That's where young Sean came in. He took the old man round the horse sales and picked out a couple of beauties, put them into training for him. Won just about everything there was to win, round here anyways."

"He had a way with horses then?"

"You could say that, yes," Reg paused and frowned as he looked into the bottom of his empty glass.

"Another drink, Reg?"

"Ooh that would be marvellous, I'll have a pint of best ale, seeing as you're offering!"

Mick took both glasses back to the bar. "Two pints of best, please" he asked the barmaid.

"Coming up" she said, smiling. "Is Reg telling you a tale then?"

"He is, for sure. And if all an evening's entertainment costs me is a pint, then it's cheap at the price" Mick answered.

"Oh, you'll need more than the one" the barmaid warned, pulling two pints and setting their refilled glasses on the bar towel. "He can stretch out a story for hours, can Reg."

Mick smiled and took the pints back to their table. Reg beamed and thanked Mick for his generous gift.

"You were saying?" Mick guided Reg back to the story.

"Oh yes. Young Sean. Well, he served on that farm for nigh on forty years by the finish. Took a local wife and settled in the cottage across the yard from the farmhouse. Brought up a family there. Wife worked for the missis, on and off, doing sewing and cleaning and a bit of cooking."

"Helped with the kids I expect."

"Oh no. No, no. That was the thing you see. Old man and his wife had no babies at all. Not one. Many times the missis cried on Sean's wife's shoulder about it all. With her having four good strong kiddies to bring up and all. It fair broke her heart, it did."

"And then, years passed, Sean and his wife moved into the farmhouse to care for the old ones and Sean ran the farm, looked after the horses, took cattle to market, just about everything. And then one day the doctor came with his bag and sat Sean and his wife down and told them that the old man had took up with cancer and there wasn't nothing he could do. No hospital in the land could cure that, being as how far it had got, and they should just try to keep him comfortable as best they could. And then, the next week, when the old man couldn't get out of his bed no more, the lawyer was asked to visit. The men all sat around the bed and the old man told the lawyer his wishes. That Sean and his wife were to have the farm when he was gone, but that they were to carry on in the same tradition and keep the horses going. And look after his wife for as long as she had left. And that wasn't an easy thing, as she was older than her husband and had gone a bit strange herself."

"What you might say was dementia now?" Mick suggested.

"Yes. That kind of thing, wandering about the farm in her nightie and calling folks by other folks's names and the like. So, it was all made legal and Sean Nichols got the farm and everything stood on it. Nice old tractor, everything. Don't get me wrong, they did right by the old lady. The wife cared for her till she died in her arms a couple of years after the old man. Didn't want for nothing. Always well fed and the place kept warm right till the end."

"But isn't John's name Weston? Who owns the farm now, I mean."

"Oh yes, but that's another tale, son."

Mick waved to the barmaid and she shook her head, smiling, and brought over two more pints.

Reg took a long drink, a deep breath and continued.

"Well, now. Fiona's father, another John, had three children with his wife, Joanne, I think her name was. Two boys, with Fiona in the middle. They all grew up around the horses, and they was riding a little pony before they could walk. But when the boys went off to study, neither of them came home much. One of them studied law and joined some big firm in the City. The younger one was quite a talented rider, as it goes, although he never could beat Fiona, despite his having the best horses money could buy. But one summer at the weekend, he came home from college and announced over their Sunday roast dinner that he was going to Australia with his friend whose folks had a sheep ranch, near Brisbane, I think it was. There was an almighty row, and old John Nichols banging on the table and the women crying. Well, the lad up and left the farm that very day and never went back for nigh on twenty years."

"That's a bit sad for them all. I expect Fiona and her mum missed him."

"The wife missed him bad, that's true. He was always a favourite of hers. But that's when the old man had to take a long hard look at things as he wasn't getting any younger, and they had forty-two horses in training at the peak."

"Forty-two? Their muck pile must have been pretty impressive," Mick mused.

Reg chuckled. "It was, lad. You always knew where to get a bag of it for your roses."

"So, did Fiona inherit the farm after that then?"

"Well, that's where it all got interesting. Old John and his wife talked and talked about it, and the wife never understood why he couldn't accept that the lads weren't interested and just let Fiona run it, let her take the strain for a bit, and he could still help her out when she needed advice. Then they could go on holiday for once. And the old man said he'd only agree to leave it all to Fiona if she married a good man who was prepared to keep the yard going proper. And the wife said they'd never get away with choosing a husband for their daughter, but that she had a plan, if he would just listen a bit."

"A plan?" Mick was intrigued. The barmaid brought more ale without being asked. Mick handed her the cash, thanked her and let Reg carry on with his story.

Reg chuckled. "You know what women are like. Always plotting and planning something. So the wife made a list of good young men who she thought would look after the farm and be good to Fiona and old John picked young John Weston. His father was Racing Manager at one the biggest yards in the whole of Oxford and the lad seemed to have his Father's brains when it came to horses and jockeys and all that. So…" Reg paused, taking a long slow drink, smacking his lip and setting his glass down carefully before turning to Mick again. "They made sure the pair of them met up at every race meeting and horse show and get together there was going on. And when the two of them started going out together, on dates and things, her father told Fiona he wasn't having it, and said if he found out they'd been out again, the two of them, there'd be words said."

Mick looked puzzled. "But I thought they'd picked John out beforehand?"

"Oh yes, they had. But knowing what Fiona's like, well, trying to stop her was the best way to make sure they got together proper, like. And luckily for old John, they did."

"But what about the brothers? Didn't they want a share of their inheritance? That farm must be worth quite a bit."

"As it happens, they came to an agreement, and John Weston's father gave the newly weds a chunk of cash as a wedding gift. Said he'd been saving all his life and he wanted his lad to have the best, and it was the least he could do. And the brother that went to

Australia, turns out he married his best friend and they started a guest house as a sideline on the sheep farm, and made enough to put down the deposit on another old wreck in the town. Did it up and did the same again. Worked their arses off for twenty years, and now they got a whole chain of them."

"The other was rich enough not to care much, but said if his children wanted to ride or get involved, could Fiona accommodate them, in return for keeping the farm together, like."

"Well that sounds like a job well done. Makes sense why Fiona rules the roost then. If the farm was really hers."

"It's not that simple though. You see, when Fiona found out what her parents had done, she was furious and threatened to call it all off and let her father find someone else to run the yard. And old John and his wife didn't want young John Weston finding out they'd been plotting and him going elsewhere. There's plenty of yards would have had young John on their books. So, in the back of her mind, she knows she's only got that farm because of John. And they make it work between them, so what's the worry." Reg drained the last of his pint, banged it back on the table and smiled triumphantly at Mick. "Now young man," he said, with a slight slur in his speech, "I would be much obliged if you would see me to my door in that car of yours as I may have trouble walking that distance."

"Happy to oblige, my friend," said Mick, "walk this way." And Reg stumbled to the car leaning on Mick's arm.

More Stories

Sophie stared at her reflection in the long wood framed mirror in the tack shop. The navy jacket was shaped at the waist and made the most of her slim figure. The white jodhpurs were soft and stretchy, like wearing soft cotton tights, and the black leather boots reflected the light from the single bulb hanging in the changing room.

"How does it look?" Sophie heard Fiona's voice and almost jumped, landing back in the present with a jolt.

"It's... well it's marvellous!" Sophie replied. She tore herself away from the mirror and pushed back the curtain. Smiling, she pirouetted in front of Fiona and the shop assistant who hovered about, pretending to tidy the shelves, until Fiona asked her: "Would you mind helping us with a body protector? A medium weight one please, for a slim built rider."

"Of course, Mrs Weston, I'll bring a couple over." She hurried off looking pleased and thinking of her month end bonus. Only the best for Fiona Weston, and the best doesn't come cheap.

"Gloves," said Fiona. "We mustn't forget those." They both leaned over the stand with the gloves hung neatly in rows. Sophie picked up some grey cotton ones and checked the price.

"Not those, Sophie, these leather ones are much better," and she handed two pairs over for Sophie to try. The Small fitted perfectly. "We'll get the white ones for the dressage phase and keep the navy ones for cross country and showjumping." Fiona handed the larger ones to the shop assistant and took the body protectors from her. "Slip that jacket off Sophie, let's try these next." The jacket was put back on the hanger, and Sophie struggled into the first body protector. The girl helped her into it and walked around her, checking the length and the fit under her arms.

"I think this one's too short. It doesn't cover the spine properly. This brand does come up a bit shorter than the others. Better try this one," and she handed Sophie the next one, taking the short one from her and dropping it onto the floor while she helped Sophie with the zip. "That's a bit better, but could you just try the next size up? I think that might be perfect, but you never can be sure till you try it." The next size was fetched and Sophie squeezed into it. Fiona laughed as Sophie grimaced. "They do get softer once you've worn them a bit," she said. "It's the special padding in them, it moulds to your body with the warmth."

"Does it? I feel like I'm dressed up in a tyre. How do you even ride in these things?"

"As carefully as if you weren't wearing it at all," Fiona answered. "We'll take that as well, if you think it's the right fit?"

"Oh yes, that's the right one. See how it comes a bit further down but not far enough to interfere with the back of the saddle. And it's close fitting, but with enough clearance under the arms so you can still move..."

"You can?" Sophie took off the body protector and handed it to the girl, who gathered it up with the gloves, jacket and the box for the boots and made her way to the till. Sophie went back into the changing room and took one last look at the shiny black boots, the blinding white shirt and stock, and the white jodhpurs and folded them carefully before putting on her jeans and work trainers to join Fiona at the till.

"That will be £485 and ninety pence please, Mrs Weston," the girl said, smiling, placing the new clothes carefully packed in huge carrier bags onto the counter. Fiona handed over her card, tapping in the number and took the receipt as Sophie picked up the bags and made her way out of the shop and put them onto the back seat of the landrover before climbing into the passenger seat.

"Well that was a successful trip. We managed to get everything we needed in the one place. I'm glad we won't have to make another trip into Stow." Fiona put the vehicle into reverse and looked behind her. Glancing at Sophie she asked: "It all seemed to fit nicely? What do you think?"

"It's all beautiful. Those jodhpurs are like wearing fresh air, and I could hardly tell I had that jacket on either."

"It's worth getting the best, might cost a bit more but it makes such a difference to your ride when you can concentrate without anything rubbing or restricting what you're trying to do. It's amazing how looking the part helps your confidence."

"Yes. Thank you for buying it all. It really is lovely stuff."

Fiona smiled as she turned the landrover out of the car park and onto the road. "I'm glad you're pleased. You looked a million dollars, I must say." They picked up speed and settled to a steady sixty miles an hour on the dual carriageway. Sophie looked out of the window, watching the hedges and fields flash past. They were quiet for a while. Fiona broke the silence.

"I hope you don't mind me asking, but.. well.... Maureen said you'd had... an accident... when you were young. With a horse..."

"Oh yes. It's not a secret. But it wasn't a riding accident, not really. We were..."

"You don't have to talk about it if you don't want to, of course. I was just interested in how people cope. You know, when stuff happens."

"Yes. It was tough for a while. I was lucky my mum looked after my pony. I didn't even go to the yard for months."

"Really? It must have been very difficult."

"It was. The owner was fine about it, after they'd got over the shock of course."

"So it wasn't your horse then?"

"No. And they sued the driver. But the money means nothing when you lose the best horse you ever owned." Fiona glanced in the mirror as she started her turn off the dual carriageway. Then at Sophie.

"I'd just got the horse going out on hacks. The owners sent him to me to start his training as they'd never backed a youngster before. I'd done a few by then, even though I was still a teenager. But that day, it was windy so I decided we'd just walk. He was on his toes for a while but soon settled. He was jogging along beside me nicely and then the car came round the corner. The driver had been drinking and was too far over. I fell into the ditch, but the horse was hit full sideways on. He had to be put to sleep on the roadside. They vet said his injuries were likely to be extensive. Internal. And one of his forelegs was badly broken." Sophie stared straight in front, her eyes moist. A tear rolled down her cheek. She sniffed.

"I'm so sorry. I had no idea. It really wasn't your fault. There was nothing you could have done."

"No. We were just in the wrong place at the wrong time. Luckily the landlord at the pub testified that the driver had been in the pub all afternoon. The police were all over it. They said I was lucky to be alive. And I suppose that's right. But it didn't feel like it at the time. And for months after."

"Oh God, that's awful. Poor you!"

"My mum knew one of those sports coaches, and she talked it all through with me and told me what I was feeling was all normal, and that helped a bit."

"Yes. I can see that would help. There's some very good people out there these days. How did you get back into horses after that?"

"Well, it was hard, but the horse that got… killed… the owners bought another one from the same yard and asked me if I'd work with her too. I just point blank refused at first, but they were a lovely couple of people and told me they didn't blame me at all, and I shouldn't let one stupid driver take away my gift."

"Your gift. Yes."

"I pleaded with them, to find someone else. But they kept insisting. And my mum persuaded me to at least try. She was a lovely mare. A Trakehner thoroughbred cross. Nearly black, with two white socks behind. I worked with her, took her to her first show and then handed her back. They went on the show her at County level. In working hunter classes. Did very well too."

"For what it's worth, I think your mum was right. And those owners. And now we get the benefit." Fiona turned the car onto the drive, pulled on the handbrake and turned the key. After a few moments silence Sophie turned to her employer and asked: "Do you... think about Meg?"

"Oh yes, every day. She was the best horse I ever sat on. Tried her heart out in everything. She was the last horse my dad ever bought. She wasn't much to look at when she came home. A gangly yearling but we did everything together. Did all the intermediate level shows..." her voice tailed off. "Oh listen to us. These are the things that have made us who we are. We shouldn't complain. It's just life."

Sophie smiled gently. "You're right."

"Let's get those new clothes hung up before they look like we got them from a jumble sale."

"Pretty expensive jumble sale if we did!" Sophie said. They both laughed.

Field Farm

One morning Joe and I knew something different was going to happen. We were fed earlier than usual and had much more brushing done and our tack was nowhere to be seen. Normally it is hung over the stable door ready while we are brushed and tidied up and our rugs removed. On weekdays, after the racehorses have gone to the gallops, we are quickly brushed over and our tack is put on then we wait for Fiona and make our way to the arena together, me, Joe, Maureen, Sophie and Fiona. But today John brought the horse box to the gate and let down the big door at the back. Maureen came to me first. 'Come on old boy," she said, as she clipped the lead rope onto my headcollar, "time to see what you're made of." And she led me out of my stable across the yard. I was always first onto the horsebox and Maureen led me to the far end and tied the rope to the ring. She was about to leave and go and fetch Joe, but I was worried on my own away from Joe and danced about so my feet made a noise like thunder and John shouted something from the tack room. He didn't sound pleased, so Fiona said Maureen should stay and she'd get Joe. With Joe by my side again everything was alright and we both settled to eat our hay, sending the brightly coloured haynets swinging on their short length of baler twine as we pulled the fresh hay through the holes.

"Sophie? Ah there you are!" Fiona called as Sophie came out of the tack room in her jodhpurs and jacket. "Have you got the body protector? They won't let you ride without it, you know, and we don't want a wasted journey."

"Oh crikey, no!" she said and ran back to the tack room to fetch it. Maureen lifted the door at the back of the horse-box and Fiona shut the bolts on her side. When we were safely shut in, Fiona said: "Right, we'll see you there. John's going to come and see how they go. And look at how the jumps are made." Sophie and Maureen smiled at each other and when they climbed up into the cab Maureen said 'That's his next job sorted then. Set of cross country jumps in the bottom field."

"Let's hope she doesn't want a water jump. She'll have him carrying buckets down there." They both laughed as Maureen swung the lorry round onto the road.

Our journey was not very long, and when we arrived and stepped out of the horse box there were not many horses or people, not like a show. We walked about getting used to our surroundings until Fiona came over with John by her side. "We'll just have a walk first, let them see the jumps, then make a plan," she said. So Joe and I were led along the edge of a large field with hedges all around it. Sophie led Joe and Maureen walked beside me. There were lots of obstacles along the edge and at various places in the field, some were large and came up to our chests, whilst others were smaller, like logs. They were not brightly coloured, like show jumps, which we were used to, but these were mostly wood and we could not see through them. As we turned the corner at the bottom of the field there was a large pond with rails either side and one of the other sides was a longer gentler slope with sand. As we walked past it I stretched out my neck to sniff the surface of the water as the sun reflected from it. Maureen stopped and stood quietly beside me as I investigated.

"Joe, what is this?" I asked.

"Just water I think" Joe replied.

"How deep?"

"Can't tell. Try!"

So I pawed at the water with my foot. It wasn't deep at all. I took a step and stretched my neck out even further. Joe followed as we both stepped into the water up to the top of our hooves. I pawed again and splashed Joe who skipped sideways and leapt into the middle of the water making a tiny wave which lapped at the sandy edges of the pond. Sophie lost her footing, tripped and let go of Joe's reins and Maureen reached out to grab her and let go of me.

"Run!" I shouted and we plunged through the middle of the pond and out the other side with white foam spraying all around. Running up the hill was fun but hard work and we eventually slowed to a trot and circled round until we saw Fiona and John who caught our reins and brought us both to a halt.

"You ok girls?" John shouted as Maureen and Sophie ran up the hill to rejoin them.

"Yes, fine thanks. Bit wet though. Sorry about that" Maureen panted, as she stopped beside us and bent over to catch her breath. Sophie rejoined us and took my rope from John who smiled and winked.

"Well, they don't seem to have a problem with water," he said, helpfully, turning to Fiona who looked like a cloud full of thundery rain. "And it's a good job they did that before you got on or I reckon you two would have wet arses by now."

"Oh John," Fiona began crossly and then she shook her head and smiled.

And then we learnt what it means to do cross-country.

***

That afternoon, after our trip to Field Farm Joe and I stood in our stables with our heads over the half doors watching everyone coming and going.

"Out of all our work, I think I liked that the best," I said to Joe.

"Yes, that water was fun! It was so good to run free for a while. The humans can't run very fast at all can they?"

"No. Not at all. Is that why they want us? So they can go faster?"

"I expect so," Joe replied, "And they'd never jump those fences like we can."

"No. I knocked my knee on one of them, you know. It doesn't hurt much now though."

"Tuck your feet up more next time."

"Yes. I will."

Field Farm Again

The time came around quite quickly when we were taken to Field Farm again. This time it was just the girls and Fiona. John said he'd seen enough and would get some plans for the solid jumps and start building straightaway.

Sophie had her older riding gear on, and her and Fiona helped each other into their body protectors. We were about to start on our walk around and another rider appeared. There wasn't a horsebox so this horse must have lived somewhere quite near. The rider seemed to know Fiona.

"Morning. Nice to see you, Mrs Weston. How are they this morning?' the rider said as he stopped his horse near to us.

"Very well thank you. We're going to do a time trial today, in preparation for the one day event next month."

"Marvellous!" replied the rider. "Which class?"

"Just the entry level. It's their first time at a proper event. Slowly does it."

"Oh yes. There's no rush. Isn't that your showjumping mare's colt? The one by Meadow Valley Dancer?"

"It is. And Joe is one of John's racers who needed a change of career."

They chatted for a short while. Joe ate the grass and I stayed close by his side. The rider's horse stood uncomfortably, lifting his head and fidgeting. His mouth was kept closed by the straps of the noseband he wore.

"Right. Let's get on then," Fiona announced. "Have you got the stopwatch Maureen?"

"Right here," she replied. "I'll start you off at the bottom right?"

"Yes, once we've warmed up. Let's have a trot round and a canter through the woods before we start. Ready Sophie?"

Sophie nodded and smiled. She led Joe to the mounting block and was quickly aboard. Maureen gave Fiona a leg up and we were ready. I pranced a little, eager to get going.

"Steady on, old boy," said Maureen as she quickly tightened my girth and nodded to Fiona and we moved off together, Joe and me, trotting along the grass track round the side, with the morning sun glinting through the trees.

"There's been a bit of rain overnight, so we'll need to watch the ground through the woods, said Fiona. "We don't want any accidents. We'll have a canter through there and check it's going to be safe. If it's too wet we'll have to stick to the main track."

"Okey dokey," replied Sophie.

We had our canter through the woods and although the ground was left with our hoofprints, it wasn't so soft that we would lose our footing. We met Maureen with her stop watch at the ready.

After a short break Fiona said; "OK, here we go then. I'll go first, Joe needs to be a fair distance back, but match my pace. The only fast gallop is before and after the last, but it's a fair sized log, so steady if you need to."

Sophie didn't seem to hear. She sat quietly, reins loose, breathing deeply, gazing between Joe's ears. Joe stood like a rock, but I could tell he was ready to run as soon as he got the signal from his rider. Fiona watched them for a moment, and Sophie turned, aware of everyone's eyes on her turned and smiled. "I'm ready," she said.

We had a wonderful run that day. I wanted to gallop fast, but Fiona kept me steady with gentle pressure on the bit which stopped as soon as I listened and slowed a little. The jumps were not as big as the ones we did at home, but they were solid and I remembered to tuck my knees up higher. I was a little reluctant at first, but there was Joe, a short distance behind me.

Through the woods we had to go slower as the ground was heavy and it was harder work. Joe was far enough back not to have mud in his face but he kept up a steady pace behind me. The logs came up quickly and it was harder to see in the shade of the enormous oak trees. Then over a ditch and out into the sunshine again.

We dropped into the water complex and Fiona let the reins slip through her fingers so I could steady myself as my feet hit the soft sandy bottom and the white spray made the hair on our legs and belly shiny and slick as we cantered out and up the slight hill to where I could see Maureen with her papers, sitting on a camping chair. Fiona encouraged me on with her hands well forward and a gentle nudge at my sides. I stretched out my legs and the ground was a blur as we cleared the last fence at full gallop and thundered to the finishing point.

"Woahhhhh..."said Fiona, as we circled round the horse box and trotted back to Maureen and Joe.

Maureen was busy writing down her figures. Sophie dismounted and patted Joe's neck, grinning. Joe and me were both breathing hard, but Joe soon got his breath back and dropped his head to eat the grass. Fiona jumped down and removed her helmet. She blew a stray lock of hair from her eyes.

"How did we do?" she asked Maureen, as she loosened my girth and ran the stirrups up the leathers.

Maureen gazed at her paper chewing the end of her pencil.

"I'll have to check it, but I think you were inside the time. A bit quick if anything."

"That's not a problem, the course was a bit shorter than we'll be doing, so I'd expect them to slow a bit at the full length."

"Yes, over about 1500m, you were... 456 metres per minute," Maureen announced proudly, passing the little notebook to Fiona.

"Marvellous!" Fiona exclaimed. "Better than I thought. Another couple of goes and we'll be spot on! Lets get them cooled off and back home. And, Sophie?"

Sophie had taken off Joe's saddle and bridle and was putting on his cooler rug. She glanced over her shoulder.

"That was very well ridden. How did it feel?"

"Oh, he was amazing. Very steady over everything and got into a nice rhythm. Plenty of gallop left at the end. I think he could easily have gone round again!"

Fiona beamed. She patted my neck and got a sweet from her pocket for me and handed the packet to Maureen. Joe lifted his head from the grass when he heard the rustle of paper.

"Well, I'll see you back at the yard. Thanks girls." And she handed my reins to Maureen, pulled off her gloves and headed back towards her car.

"When she says 'we'd better get them cooled off', she means us," Maureen commented, as she led me back towards the horse box where Sophie had my rug ready. She removed my saddle, threw the rug over my back, did up the straps and rubbed my forehead gently.

"Of course. The Royal We!" Sophie replied.

Frustrations

Some days were more difficult than others. Standing in our stables for many hours a day is not an easy thing for a horse. Some days we just look out at the busy goings-on of the yard, horses coming and going, people talking and sharing jokes together as they provide our food and water. But as the days began to get shorter that year I found I could not concentrate on my work so well.

One day we were taken to the arena as usual and Maureen led me about, checking my saddle and brushing a stray bit of straw from my mane until Fiona arrived. Joe was with me, as always, and even he seemed less cheery than usual. Today we were to practice our dressage test. This is when we have to walk, trot and canter around, changing direction at different spots, stopping neatly in the middle at the end, where we began. It is hard work, bending and stretching, turning and stopping and though I tried I could not find the enthusiasm to do my best. After a few minutes Fiona brought me to the short side of the arena, where Joe, Maureen and Sophie watched and waited.

"He just doesn't feel right today. What do you think, girls?" Fiona asked.

"Well, he's stepping through OK, and keeping his balance nicely round the corners, but there's definitely something missing," Maureen agreed.

"Any change in his eating habits? Anything like that?"

"No, nothing major. He has taken longer to eat his food recently, maybe, but usually it's because he's too busy watching what someone else is doing."

Fiona smiled and leaned forward to pat my neck. "That's our Malé" she said. "I'll just try and wake him up a bit, but if he's not up for it, we'll give Joe a try, then call it a day. I hope he's not coming down with something." She sounded quite worried, but there was nothing I could do to tell her what was wrong.

Fiona asked me to trot down the long side. She nudged my sides to ask me to stretch, then at the corner she sat down lightly in the saddle and asked for me to canter. A few things happened all at once. Fiona tapped me lightly with her long thin whip. A bird flew out of the hedge. I dodged away from the bird. Fiona's hands jerked at the reins and I felt a brief, searing pain in my mouth. Then I ran. I ran and bucked and Fiona landed on the sandy surface. I skidded around the arena bucking and rearing, reins and stirrups flying. Joe whinnied and although I only vaguely heard him I remembered that he was my friend. My best friend in all the world. The one who had been by my side since we were taken from our mothers as tiny foals. Sophie hurried to my side with Joe. Maureen ran over to Fiona. She groaned and rolled over, hands pressing her back.

"I'll get John," Sophie said as she ran past with Joe and me trotting either side of her. One of the jockeys was leaning on the tack room door, checking his phone when we got to the yard and Sophie handed us both to him.

114

"Sort these two out would you, Tig? Need to get John. Fiona's had a fall."

"Shit," he said. "John's in the office. What happened?"

"Malé had a bit of a strop, that's all. Don't think it's anything serious," she said as she ran to the farmhouse.

Tig put me in my stable and Joe in his. I flinched as he took off my bridle.

"Woah there Malé, let's have a little look at that mouth of yours shall we? Ah, I see what's happened. Did it hurt ya then old boy? You've got yerself a fine cut there. But never mind, it will soon heal. I'll get Maureen to put something on that from her box of tricks. Soon have you right as rain fella." He patted my neck and I stood for a moment with my head close to him. I had not meant to hurt anyone.

John strode across the yard and swung open the gate to the track which led to the arena. Fiona was half way up when he caught up with her. "What the hell happened? Are you OK?" He went to her side and supported her along with Maureen, as she hobbled back to the yard grimacing with every step.

"Let's get you home and I'll call the doctor."

"There's no need. I'm fine." Fiona protested.

"Well you don't look fine. Just to be on the safe side."

"They won't come out now. It can wait till the morning. You can run me to the surgery then. You don't make this much fuss if a jockey has a fall."

"Jockeys are always falling off. They're used to it. And I'm not married to any of them."

Fiona smiled and grimaced at the same time. "Glad to hear it!" she croaked.

Inside the farmhouse John sat Fiona slowly in the armchair and sat on the arm, holding her hand.

"Can I get you anything?"

Fiona pressed her head into his side and wept.

"My back. It really hurts… Must have fallen funny… "

"It's OK… I'll get you some paracetamol in a minute. You'll be fine. Don't worry," John soothed.

Soon, Fiona took one final sob and sniffed. John reached over to the dresser and passed her a box of tissues. She blew her nose and sniffed again. Then she took a deep breath.

"Can you ask Maureen to pop in please? Or Sophie?"

John frowned. "As long as it's not to discuss alterations to your training programme!" he tried to sound stern. "You're not riding again until the doctor's been, and that's final."

Fiona smiled weakly. "Well, it kind of was," she said, "but actually I want them both turning out for a week while I recover a bit. Malé just isn't right. And you know how they go off their work sometimes. They just need a break and them come back fresh again. It won't interrupt their schedule much."

"And if it does, that's just hard luck." John got up and went into the kitchen. "What do you want to take your tablets?" he called through to Fiona.

"Oh, water, and then coffee please."

"I'll put some fresh on. The girls can have a cup too."

John put fresh coffee in the filter, swilled out the coffee maker's glass pot, filled the machine with water from the jug and switched it on.

He returned to Fiona's side and placed the two white tablets and a glass of water on the small table beside her, moving a copy of the Racing Times and some bills first. Fiona swallowed them, grimacing again. She sat with the glass in her lap, staring into it. John watched her carefully for a moment, then stood up. "I'll go and fetch the girls," he said.

Maureen was in my stable with Sophie when John arrived.

"How is he?" he asked, leaning over the half door. "Ah! Your box of tricks."

Maureen had a grey box with a metal clasp on the top. It was full of small bottles of creams and sprays to help the horses with minor injuries and bottles with strong smells to help horses who had trouble settling.

Maureen turned. "Oh, he's got a cut in his mouth from the bit. It'll be a bit sore for a while but I've put some of this salve on it to numb it while it starts to heal. Should be fine in a couple of days." She put the tiny bottle back in her box, snapped the lid shut and patted my neck. Sophie stood at my head and I rested my muzzle in her hands.

"So, we won't need to get the vet out then?" John sounded pleased.

Maureen smiled. "No, not this time." Sophie unclipped the rope from my headcollar and leaned her face on mine for a second, then she and Maureen left my stable.

"Could you pop into the farmhouse for a chat with Fiona? She wants to discuss an altered training plan, you know what she's like, but no riding till we've had the doctor out, OK?"

"Of course," said Maureen, "I'll just pop this back in the tack room."

"Just go straight in, she's in the lounge," and John strode off to find Tig, who was snoozing in the one comfy chair in the staff kitchen.

"As if Fiona would even listen to us!" Sophie said as they went through the gate to the farmhouse garden.

"You can't blame him for trying," she said, "he's probably hoping that girl power thing will prevail. Anyway, I've got a plan."

"You have?" Sophie replied, unsurprised, as they took off their yard boots in the porch. "It had better be a good one."

"It is, but you never know with Fiona. Just back me up, alright?"

"Depends," Sophie answered, but Maureen had already opened the farmhouse door and called "It's only us, shall we come in?" Sophie followed without further discussion.

"Come in girls, there's coffee, help yourselves" Fiona called back.

Settled with a mug of strong fresh coffee in front of them, Maureen asked "how are you feeling?"

"My back is caning, if I'm honest, possibly cracked my pelvis a bit, but I'm hoping it's just a bruised tailbone or something. I'll get to the chiropractor once the pain's died down a bit. How's Malé?"

"He's fine. Had quite a cut on the left side of his mouth, but I've put some salve on it and he seems OK."

Fiona winced as she shifted her weight in the armchair. Maureen pursed her lips. "When's the doctor coming?"

"Oh, don't you start. I've got John wanting the get the air ambulance out!" she tried to smile. "I'll get him to call later today. Now, about Malé and Joe."

"Yes," Maureen interrupted, "I was thinking they might need a bit of a break. They've been training most days since March. Would it be worth giving them a few days off till you're back and fit?"

Fiona actually looked relieved. She looked thoughtfully at Maureen for a second. "Yes, I think you're right. Malé is just like Meg. These stressy types need to let off steam once in a while. It's the price you pay for their talent, I suppose. What do you suggest?"

"Well, there are a couple of options. They could both go in the paddock with the oldies, or there's the latest batch of weanlings. They could have a few days with them. That should take their mind off things. And there's more room for them to stretch their legs in the big field."

"Hmmm…. I don't think John would want them in with the weanlings, at least not till the mares have gone back. With Malé being entire and all that."

"How about in with the oldies, then in the mare's field when they've gone? We can fetch them in every night if you like."

"Yes, that sounds like a plan. I think they'll enjoy that. And then we can revisit it once the doctor's been. Sophie, what do you think?"

"Me? Oh, err, yes, they would both benefit from some time off. Even Joe has felt a bit down recently, and he's the eternal optimist."

"Yes, he's been marvellous. We wouldn't have got so far without him, but it's time for a break. Definitely."

Maureen smiled and got up to go, "That's settled then. We'll get them turned out this afternoon for a few hours and I'll bring them in this evening."

"Before you go..." Fiona half turned in her chair and winced again. "In that drawer in the dresser, second one down, there's some pain killers. Could you pass them to me please. I'll put them in my pocket. I can do without John fussing."

Maureen glanced through the lounge towards the kitchen window. It was all clear, so she rummaged around in the drawer and found a packet of tablets with the silver foil back printed with black writing. Half the tablets were gone. Maureen passed them over. "These?" she asked.

"Yes. Thanks." she glanced at them and pushed them into the inside pocket of her fleece jacket. "Keep me updated on Malé and Joe, will you?"

"Of course," Maureen assured her. "A bit of a break won't do them any harm," and she turned to go.

Sophie followed. "If you need anything, you know where we are," she said, and they both made their way out of the farmhouse, closing the wooden door quietly behind them. Fiona heaved a sigh, and even though she closed her eyes tightly, the tears ran down her face and onto her hands.

***

We knew something was different when Maureen and Sophie came out of the farmhouse, as the staff don't often go in there. Meetings and discussions are had in the larger tack room upstairs from the kitchen. We can hear them talking and smell the smoke as it drifts out of the open window, and the jockeys laugh at each other's jokes until John arrives and then they are quiet.

I wondered if we were going back to the arena to finish our work, and my heart sank for a moment, but no. We just had our headcollars on. Maybe we were going onto the horse-walker, where we have to walk slowly round and round and round. No, it wasn't that either as the horse-walker is behind the stable block and we were being led the other way. I whinnied to Joe who was slightly ahead of me. He turned his head and whinnied back.

We were led down the main track past the car park, along the hedge under the big chestnut trees where a gentle breeze made the leaves drip drops of silver rainwater onto us as we passed, on to the paddock by the road, furthest from the house.

"Oh Joe!" I said. "The paddock!" Joe tossed his head. The retired geldings lifted their heads and watched as the girls led us through the gate. I could hardly stay still and as soon as our lead ropes were unclipped Joe and me swung on our hind legs away from the gate. "Run!" I shouted, and Joe and me were off, galloping away from the gate as fast as our legs could take us. We bucked and reared and pretended to fight, waving our front legs in the air, turning and bucking and dodging each other until we stood snorting and tossing our heads at the far end of the field, breathing hard after our exertion. The older geldings came over and sniffed us, greeting us like old friends. Perhaps they were bored in the field on their own, as they seemed happy to see us.

Soon we dropped our heads to eat the short fresh grass. It tasted so good after eating hay most of the time. I soon forgot the sore patch in my mouth, and later we dozed under the chestnut tree. Joe and me, just like it used to be.

Sophie and Maureen stood at the gate for a while.

"Do you think they enjoy it?" Sophie mused, her foot resting on the bottom rung of the wooden field gate, arms draped over the top of it.

"Enjoy what?" Maureen answered watching us graze alongside each other, the sun still strong for the time of year.

"Work. All that being ridden and stabled and stuff."

"Well, they look happy right now."

"I know they do now, but…"

"They were bred to be working horses. They don't know any different. They get the best of everything."

"I know, but… do you ever wonder what they think about it all?"

"No. They're horses. They don't really think like we do. As long as they're well fed and safe, I don't think it matters that much to them at all."

"It's all so unnatural though. So far from what wild horses live like."

"Yes, but at least they don't have to worry about being eaten by coyotes."

Sophie turned towards Maureen and smiled. "You know what I mean."

"I do," Maureen replied, "but without it all, you and me would be without a job between us."

Sophie sighed, gazing across the paddock at four horses, strolling about, nibbling on the grass and swishing their tails at the flies. "I know, but… if it could just be a bit more natural for them. A bit more tuned in to how they like things."

"Soph, we have to do things how Fiona likes them, remember. They're not our horses. We don't make the decisions."

"So, what was your plan? Was this it? To get Fiona to let them have some time off?" Sophie turned to her friend, an enquiring look on her face.

"Oh that. Yes. They needed a break, and luckily, so does Fiona right now. She's not going to be doing any riding for a week or so, I'll bet. She was in a lot more pain than she was letting on. You saw the way she fell, right on her left hip."

"Yes. I saw. She looked in agony. What were those tablets she got you to find?"

"The ones that John has for when jockeys hurt themselves and don't want the doctor to know about it."

"Oh, them. Tig said they were some kind of mild morphine things. He had a couple when he came off at Chepstow and a horse caught his ankle with its foot. Said he was away with the fairies and smiled his way through the doctor's visit."

"Yep. And not so mild either."

"Crikey," Sophie said. "Do you think she'll go all soft on everyone now then?"

"They're painkillers not a personality transplant, Soph," Maureen grinned.

"You can't say that about our employer's wife!" Sophie gasped in mock horror.

"Just did!" Maureen replied. They both laughed as they turned back up the track to the stables, leadropes over their shoulder until it was time for us to come in for the night.

***

After our doze, Joe and me yawned and stretched, Joe rubbed his face on his front leg and pretended to nibble my neck.

"It's so good to be free. How long do you think we'll be here, Joe?" I asked.

"I don't know, so let's make the most of it while we can."

"Yes," I replied. We watched as the sun disappeared behind a passing cloud, until the cloud was gone and the sun shone on our coats and we could feel its warmth right down to our bones.

"Joe? I have just realized something."

"What?"

"We never have choices any more. About anything. Ever."

"What do you mean?"

"I mean, the humans get to decide. All the time. What we eat, what we wear, where we go. We have metal on our feet, our hair is clipped off, we stand in our cages all day until we are wanted, then back we go again afterwards."

Joe was silent.

"We just never get to be horses any more. I like to please the humans, you know that, like my mother taught me, but sometimes… well…. It's all just too much."

The older geldings had quietly joined us. The four of us stood for a while under the trees as the sun turned orange and the air became cooler, blowing across the valley, making the leaves whisper as it passed.

"I know Malé," Joe said. "But you have me. And I have you. And that will have to be enough."

Silks

"Alright everyone, quiet please. Here's the plan for this week," John moved to stand in front of the whiteboard facing the jockeys, stable hands and his main driver Jeff. Sophie and Maureen had been asked to attend.

"Now, as you know, we have four runners at the next meet and two are in to win Mike, you'll take Darcy, the syndicate horse in the two-thirty….," a jeer broke out and a couple of the stable hands punched Mike's arm playfully. John pursed his lips, suppressing a smile.

"Aw boss, can't I ride for Simpsons?" Mike protested mildly, glad for the ride, but not for the silks he'd be wearing.

"I think you look smashing in pink, Mike, don't listen to them."

"I'll listen when they start making sense."

"It'll match your undies, Mike!"

"His undies are silk? Who'd have thought it?"

"How do you know so much about his undies?"

John smiled. "OK, OK, settle down! Then Martin, at 3pm, you're up on Radio Star. He missed his last outing with a touch of colic, but he's bounced back fine and is our best chance on the day, as long as he travels ok and we can keep him quiet. I've booked the end block where it's a bit quieter, and Sophie?"

All eyes turned to her. "I want you to get him prepped. We're still well up the ranks for best turned out and there aren't that many meetings left. If we take the top prize, I make that just under £200 for each of you. So, there's a lot resting on this."

"No pressure then," Maureen said, glancing at Sophie.

"Yes, boss," Sophie said.

"Good girl. Now, Mike, the ground will likely be firm on the day, unless we have more rain, and I don't want that filly coming in lame, so expect to take it steady. I've put the overnight rota up on the board, so make sure you've all seen it. It's going to be a big meet, with crowds, so keeping them calm is going to be top priority. Any questions?"

Various murmurs and nods, then John thanked them all and turned to go, pulling his smartphone out of his pocket as it rang and answering with "Lower Barn Farm, John Weston speaking. Ah, hello, Mr Francis, nice to hear from you… yes, yes, she's doing fine…. Of course. We'll be there to meet you at the racecourse. Yes, of course….. Thank you. I'll see you Saturday, then. Bye.. Bye.."

"The syndicate owner?" Mike asked.

"Yes," John replied, "they'll be over at the course to see Darcy run Saturday."

"No change of plan about the silks then?"

"No chance, mate. They chose it for the women. And they're our best customer right now, three horses in training and another one planned for next season, so if they choose pink, it's pink you'll have to wear," John pressed his lips together and almost winked.

"OK boss. Pink it is then."

"Absolutely." John turned and strode from the room.

Options

"Steady as she goes," Jeff strolled towards the back of the best horse box as the last horse, a tall chestnut colt was led up the ramp to the last stall, the rope swapped and the clip attached, padded partition swung across and secured.

"That's the lot then," Tig said, and made his way to the tack room for his bag before climbing up into the passenger seat of the cab. Jeff did some final checks, a horse whinnied and stamped from inside.

"Right let's get going then. Next stop Chepstow for you my lovelies."

***

Maureen slowed the car as they approached the roundabout, crossing her hands to turn the wheel, positioning the car in the right hand lane.

"Not far now. I reckon we'll be there in another five," she commented as they waited for a smart silver painted horse box to pass.

Sophie looked up from her phone. "Wait," she said. "Look at that!"

"What?" Maureen glanced in Sophie's direction, craning her neck to the left, watching for a space in the stream of Saturday evening traffic.

"There! That board. Go round again!"

"What?" Maureen pulled forwards into the centre lane.

"Go round the roundabout. I need to see what's on that board." Sophie demanded.

"Soph, we're due at the course in seven minutes!"

"It won't take an hour. Just once round! Please!"

"Jaysus…. " Maureen swung the car back into the middle lane, circling past the exit they had just come from, swearing as the driver behind them leaned on the horn and gesticulated.

"There it is! I knew it!"

"If you knew it then why have we got to take a second look?" Maureen indicated left and got back onto the dual carriageway towards the race course.

"Thanks Maur. It was an advert."

"If I've just risked our lives for a lipstick advert I'm never taking you anywhere again."

"Lipstick? What would I do with that? It was an advert for a demonstration evening. It's… wait… the 17th. That's tonight. I'm going to look it up." She fiddled intensely with her phone as Maureen glanced at the sat nav and moved across to the near side lane to approach the staff entrance to the race course. "Yes! And it's just down the road from the course. Oh My God. We've got to go."

"A demonstration? I'm sure I can't be arsed, Soph. What if you get arrested? That's your career down the pan."

"Arrested? Why would I get arrested? And anyway, how many jockeys that you know have never got arrested, and they still have a career. Oh!" Sophie giggled. "Not that kind of demonstration, a horsey one. Anyway, I think I left my placard at home this time."

"Well that's a relief. Have you got the paperwork?"

"Oh. Yeh." Sophie rummaged in the rucksack at her feet. She pulled out a brown envelope and shook it so all the papers fell into her lap.

"Any time today, Soph," Maureen muttered as the steward leaned towards the open driver's window. "This guy looks like he has the worst halitosis…"

Flicking through them quickly, Sophie found two blue cards and handed them to Maureen, who had pressed the switch so the passenger's window slid smoothly down as the steward leaned towards them.

"Thank you, ladies, that all looks in order, turn right after the barrier and make your way to the Staff Car Park and the steward will direct you there."

"Thanks, we will!" Maureen answered as she put the car in gear and moved slowly off, turning towards the car park as she had been advised.

"Halitosis? That's not very nice," Sophie turned to her friend.

"It wasn't!" Maureen answered. "Hold up, here's another one."

They were waved on up to the top end of the grass car park where another steward directed them to the next available space and checked their cards again.

"Nice day for it," the steward commented, returning their cards to Maureen. "Refreshments in the main staff restaurant from 7am."

"Thanks," Maureen smiled briefly, "Let's go there first. I could murder a cup of tea," she said, as Sophie shouldered her rucksack and Maureen got her travel bag from the back seat of the car. "Then we'll go and find Tig and the rest of the motley crew and you can sort your charges out. You'll have a job on getting them spruced up if they've sweated up in the lorry."

"Don't worry, I'll sort it," she answered as they fell into step along the path to the restaurant and joined the queue for a mug of tea.

Just in time, they arrived at the yard after dropping off their bags in their lockers as Mike and Tig were lowering the ramp.

"Sophie! Maureen! There you are. Your carriage awaits." Mike bowed slightly as Sophie smiled, passing him and making her way up the ramp to get the first horse. Although he was calm, he had sweated a little, and his neck was sleek with a shiny hand sized patch on one side. He dropped his nose into Sophie's hand and she scratched the base of his ear briefly before walking him slowly down the ramp. She led him around for a while, talking to him quietly, letting him get his bearings and take in the sounds and smells of a busy race course, horse boxes arriving one after the other. Maureen and Tig did the same, with Tig leading both of the two fillies as Mike had complained that his war wound was playing him up.

"War wound my arse," Maureen muttered.

Tig caught her words and laughed. "He was in the war, you know. Afghanistan. Did two tours back to back before he finished."

"I didn't know Mike was a soldier" Sophie commented.

"He wasn't. He was in the catering corps. And don't let him tell you otherwise."

They put the horses into the stables facing each other at the coolest end of the block, where the shade from the main building meant the horses wouldn't sweat up so much. They fetched hay and feeds, buckets, brushes and bandages, saddles and bridles, storing everything neatly in the lockup, then made sure the horses were settled for the night.

"Right, I think we're done till the morning," Maureen pulled the bolt across the stable door, shifted the kick bolt at the bottom with her foot and smiled briefly as Sophie emerged from the end stable.

"Where next?" Tig asked.

"Listen. This event that's going on. Can we go. I mean, will you come with me?" Sophie looked imploringly at Maureen.

"What kind of event is it?" Tig asked.

"It's some bunny-hugging thing Soph has found out about, damn that advertising board," Maureen replied.

"I know it's not really your thing Maur, but I can't really go on my own. I mean, I can't drive your car and.."

"And the tickets are really expensive."

"How much?" Tig interrupted.

"Yes, they are expensive, as it's on the door, but if you buy them I'll pay you back at the end of the month. I can't miss it Maur. It's Josh Bygraves. He runs a rehab place in California. All natural methods. No shoes, no stables, even rides them with no tack."

"No tack? Now that I've got to see!" Tig looked interested. Sophie turned to him.

"Oh. Will you come with me? I didn't think... well..."

"I'll try anything once," Tig smiled.

"Don't make me go Soph. I was planning on a quiet night in front of the telly with some hot chocolate."

"Where is it?" Tig asked.

"About three miles the other side of Chepstow, at the big equestrian centre."

"Too far to walk then. And how much did you say it was?"

"It's a bargain at only £25 quid a ticket!" Maureen told him.

"Jaysis, it had better be worth it. Come on Maur, let me drive Sophie over there if it means that much to her. We can slip you a fiver for the petrol."

Maureen pursed her lips together and frowned. "We've got an early start in the morning, so don't be late back," and she fished her car keys out of her pocket, handing them reluctantly to Tig with a resigned sigh. Sophie squealed and flung her arms around her friend. "Thank you! Thank you!" she said, grinning like a grand national winner. She spun around, suddenly in a fluster. "I'll get my bag. And we'll need our cards. Tig, have you got your card or we'll not get back onto site. I'll bring you loads of pictures back!" she said to Maureen over her shoulder.

"And try not to wake me up when you get in!" Maureen turned away and smiled briefly, shaking her head as the two headed off back to the car park and she made her way in the opposite direction to her room and the hot drink she'd been looking forward to.

***

"Thanks for driving, Tig," Sophie smiled as she passed Tig a can of Pepsi from her rucksack.

"No problem. I'm looking forward to it. Have you got the programme?"

"Yes," she handed it to him and leaned over as he flicked through, stopping on the double page photo of Josh Bygraves standing on the backs of two horses, a foot on each. The horses were cantering at speed, dust cloud behind them, the rider holding a rope around each of the horse's necks.

"Wow. Look at that! Do you think he'll be doing that this time?"

"I hope so, it looks like that was in an arena too."

They passed the time discussing the horses they worked with, and Tig asked about how Joe was doing.

"He's great, I think he's going to make a great eventer," she said, "He has a great gallop, but he's sensible enough to come back to you without losing the plot. And he's very laid back. I worry I'm not going to be able to pull it off, but once I'm on, Joe seems to know what it's all about, and he keeps me calm!"

"He's a good sort," Tig said. "And I think you bring the best out in each other."

"Yes, thanks," Sophie smiled as she turned to gaze at the arena. There had only been a few seats left, so they were quite high up, but at least they would be able to see everything. There was an excited buzz as people chatted, others arriving to step over each other to get to their seats in the middle of the long rows, smiling and apologizing.

At last, as Tig crushed the empty can and placed it carefully under his chair till the end, the lights dimmed and a hush fell. Spotlights beamed and swung then came to rest on the wide gates at one end. A drum roll, and the gates burst open as two horses galloped in with Josh Bygraves standing with one foot on each, whirling a rope around his head with one hand, holding the rope around the horse's necks with the other. The horses stopped in the centre, their noses level with each other, rearing in unison then standing, alert, snorting and tossing their heads.

"Good evening ladies and gentleman! Welcome to one and all. I am Josh Bygraves. And tonight I want to show you what magic can happen when you set your horses free!"

A drum roll, and Josh swung the rope around his head and then, by some invisible signal, the horses took off again, cantering side by side, followed by the spotlights strung in rows way above them. Back to the middle again, the horse halted and Josh leapt down, sending the horses away in opposite directions to gallop round the edge of the arena, joining him again in the centre. Both dropped their heads onto their outstretched front leg and bowed. The crowd laughed and clapped.

The horses pirouetted, trotted in unison, circled around Josh like a magnet, turning one way, then the other, until finally, they halted together beside him and he vaulted onto the back of the bay. They stood still again, breathing heavily as the spotlight lit up a small circle in the centre. Neither wore anything. No bit, bridle, halter or saddle. No boots or bandages, and no metal shoes.

Tig sat open-mouthed, crisp bag in one hand, untouched. Sophies eyes were bright as she leaned forward in her seat. The first performance was followed by a whole team demonstration, with horses jumping through rings, crossing each other's paths as they trotted round, dramatic music and whirling spotlights keeping everyone on the edge of their seats, until the last rider cantered out of the arena and only Josh was left.

"What you have seen tonight may seem spectacular, but we are here to tell you that any one of you can have the kind of bond with your horse that makes these things possible. Let us show you how."

And by the end, Sophie believed she could.

New directions

Sophie finished brushing the handsome chestnut horse and put the soft brush back in the bucket, swapping it for a small blue towel. She wiped the horse all over gently, talking to him often, sometimes humming quietly to herself. She finished with the towel, and stepped back, smiling. She patted the horse and held her head close to his. The horse dropped his head into her hands and blew softly.

"Soph? Sophie? You done with that horse? It's time," Maureen's voice came from the tack room. She threw the tiny saddle over the half door and swung the bridle over it. "Did you finish Darcy?"

"Yes, she's all ready. Martin's been over to see her already."

"Right, let's get them tacked up and over to the start before we miss the whole thing."

The two horse were swiftly tacked up, their stable doors swung open, and the walk to the collecting ring began. Sophie and Radio Star fell into step behind Maureen and Darcy. Sophie watched Darcy's muscular hind quarters rise and fall ahead of her as the sun shone on the quarter marks she had brushed in earlier. Each side was a large star with three smaller ones underneath, Weston's trademark. It made the horses easier to identify if the jockey's silks were obscured as they galloped in a group along the rails.

Martin was waiting in the ring and nodded and smiled at Sophie as she pulled off the lightweight rug from Radio Star's back and checked the girth.

"He looks smashing, Sophie, thanks." He checked the girth again, fiddled with the straps on his crash cap, then patted both arms in turn, frowning.

"What's up?" Sophie asked.

"My lucky sixpence. I put it in my armband. I always have it. Can't ride without that." He smiled, relieved, as he felt the coin where it had slipped down underneath his left bicep. "Phew!" he breathed. Sophie moved to the horse's offside and checked the buckles on the bridle as John appeared and gave him a leg up.

"We've had a bit of rain overnight, so the going's just about perfect. March's horse has been pulled with a suspected tendon injury, so it's as good as ours. Stay close to the rail until the final ten, then let him go. Give him a good race though. We don't want any setbacks this early on."

"Yes, boss." Martin nodded curtly and picked up the reins. John and Sophie stepped back as they began their walk to the enclosure entrance and Martin turned Radio Star to the right and stood in the stirrups as he broke into a canter to head for the start.

"Looking good, Sophie, thank you," John smiled briefly, "Just time for a cup of tea I think, then we'll head off to the winning post."

They passed the canteen and when they got to the front of the queue John leaned over the counter. "Two mugs of tea, please," he said.

"Coming up Mr Weston," the server replied, smiling.

He placed their two paper cups on the counter and John fished in his pocket for the money, hastily dumping two huge spoonfuls of sugar into his, stirring vigorously. Sophie took hers and they fell into step as they made their way to the finishing post.

"Tig said you went to that demonstration last night. Any good?" John asked, breaking stride a little to slurp his tea.

"Yes, it was amazing. I loved it." Sophie replied. "Nothing to do with racing really, but very interesting."

"They did some kind of trick riding, right?"

"Sort of," Sophie answered. "The best bit was a lovely Spanish horse doing advanced dressage moves with no tack at all. Very precise too. Made it all look easy."

"Thank god Fiona didn't go. That eventing business is dangerous enough without doing it totally naked. The horse, I meant… not Fiona… you know what I mean."

Sophie chuckled and stopped to drink her tea gratefully. She'd spent most of the day prepping the horses after a late night at the event and was beginning to feel the effects.

"How is Fiona? After the fall?"

"Oh, she's doing fine. The doctor said she hasn't broken anything, just a nasty knock to her pelvis. Couple more days and she'll be back in the saddle I expect."

"That's good."

"That reminds me, I must get some more of those painkillers." John stopped by one of the speakers as the name Radio Star blared out of it. The announcer was in full flow, it sounded like a very close finish with the favourite and Radio Star head to head in the last few furlongs. He was almost shouting when Radio Star passed the post half a head in front of the favourite.

John punched the air with one hand, spilling tea with the other. "He did it! I knew he had it in him. Let's get over there." John took one last gulp of tea and flung the cup into the nearest waste bin. Sophie followed suit and ran to catch him up as he strode into the winners enclosure beaming, as Martin unsaddled the horse for weighing in.

Maureen was at the horse's head and threw his cooler rug over his shoulders and quickly settled it straight, buckling the front as Radio Star shook his head and stamped a hind foot as sweat trickled over his fetlock.

"Hang on, good boy…. I'll get to that in a second… steady now…" Maureen spoke reassuringly to the horse rubbing his face with a damp towel and moving around to flick a fly from his belly. Sophie arrived to hold the horse's head and Maureen smiled briefly as she wiped the horse down with her small blue towel. His sides still heaved, but he was recovering fast. He rubbed his face against Sophie and she wiped the sweat and rubbed his ears gently with another towel.

Back from the weigh in, and a cheer went up as the results were announced. "First, number three, Radio

Star, owned and trained by John Weston, and ridden by Martin O'Grady...." No-one heard the rest as Radio Star was led into position at first place. Martin rejoined the group and John grabbed his hand, shook it vigorously and slapped his best jockey on the back. Everyone smiled, photos were taken. A steward came forward and spoke to John, who bent to hear him above the noise of the crowd. He beamed again and beckoned to Sophie, now waiting behind the barrier. She ducked under it and was with them in a moment. The steward handed her a certificate and an envelope and shook her hand. More photos. Then it was time to get Radio Star cooled down and back to his stable until the end of the meet when they could all go home.

New Heights

After Fiona had recovered from the fall, she came to watch us doing our daily work for a few days until she felt ready to be in the saddle again. Then, we stayed in the arena and did quite a lot of dressage movements quite often, which is not my favourite thing as it makes your neck ache after a while. But Fiona said it was where I needed to improve the most. There were some trips to Field Farm, but not so many as John had built some solid jumps around the edge of the track which went all around the farm so mostly we practiced here. It was good to gallop round and launch myself into the air right over each one and as our confidence grew, we did larger jumps with ditches and drops on the slopes. Horses as a rule, do not like ditches, as we remember that predators can hide there, but the more we practiced, the easier it became, and soon Joe and me could clear each of the jumps at their biggest height without missing a hoofbeat.

Later we did some galloping uphill and downhill, through water, balancing steadily when we went around sharp bends and were shown lots of bright objects and things that flapped so we could learn to not be afraid and to just ignore them. Fiona made sure we had some time to rest in the field and do whatever we pleased sometimes. Some days when we were free in the field, Sophie would come out and walk slowly around with us, and we would follow her about and nuzzle her pockets in case she had a sweet for us. Sometimes I thought that Sophie could understand us, even though I know that humans cannot hear what we say. Like the shadows and shapes we see at the first light of dawn, before the sun is properly risen, she sees more than most.

There were a lot more shows and events for us to attend, and the front of the horse box we travelled in began to fill with rosettes of all colours. Those days were busy and hard work for us, and on the way home Joe and me sometimes dozed as the horsebox whisked its way along lanes and motorways, swaying from side to side around the corners, and we were glad to be back home where everything was familiar and we could lie down and rest, me in the end stable and Joe in the next one.

One show day we did our dressage work in the afternoon, as it had not been such an early start as usual and we arrived as the midday March sun filtered through the clouds and made the wind bright with its thin yellow light. After this, instead of having our light rugs and travel boots put on and being led carefully back up the ramp into the horsebox, we were put into stables in a big barn, Joe next to me, as usual. Each stable had water and hay for us to eat and clean shavings on thick rubber mats, just like we had at home. But it wasn't home.

"Do you think we are going to stay here always Joe?" I asked, as the sunlight passed below the hill behind the barn and we were plunged into darkness.

"No," Joe replied, "we'll only be here until we have done the rest of our work, then they'll take us home again."

"Oh." I said, "How do you know that?"

"Because Ben told me. He's in the stable opposite. He's done this a lot of times."

I looked over the half door to see Ben, a smart grey horse we had met earlier with beautiful dapples in his coat. Ben was older than Joe and me, and his work meant he had travelled all over the country to run and jump with his rider, Nathan.

But Ben did not look happy. He rested his hind legs one after the other and as he shifted his weight from one to the other, he groaned a little. His eyes, half closed, muscled shoulders hunched a little, head hung low as he dozed. As the night wore on, and most of us woke to eat some hay I asked Ben about his life as an eventer and why he was uncomfortable.

He told me that every year was harder, with more travelling and more work, the jumps were bigger, the courses longer and the dressage more difficult.

"It was OK at first, but after a while, my joints began to hurt and I became lame at the end of the season. My humans got the vet to come and push needles into my hocks so they hurt less, but sometimes, they still do. My back too."

Another horse replied "It would be so much easier out in the pasture so you could roll and lie down and walk gently until your joints were better again."

"I am not allowed out in the pasture very much. Not until the Autumn, when my work is finished for the year," Ben replied. He dropped his head again and sighed.

Joe and me looked at each other. It was not good to hear that Ben's work had made him hurt so much. Although we sometimes caught a leg on a jump or tripped when we were learning something new, and sometimes our muscles ached after a hard day, we did not hurt all the time like Ben.

Another horse was in a larger stable across the end of the barn, and sharing with him was a beautiful horse, quite the smallest Joe and me had ever seen. His back did not even reach his friend's belly, and his mane stuck out all along his neck. I asked politely 'Excuse me, but I am wondering how does your friend manage those big jumps? His legs are so very short compared to ours."

"I can speak for myself you know!" answered Munchkin, the pony, as he reached up and pulled a mouthful of hay from the hay net tied to the rail.

Joe smiled. "Sorry, old chap, we haven't seen a horse of your size before," he answered cheerfully.

"Well I don't know where you've been all your life but there are lots of us around. I'm here to look after my friend Tom. We go everywhere together. The humans know that Tom needs me, you see. He frets if we're apart."

"I fret when Joe and me are apart!" I told him. "It's very nice to meet you."

Most of us had finished our hay when the sun came up and the sun filtered through the slats of wood above our heads, shining down on our backs so we looked like we had stripes. Some of the humans were already bustling about, greeting their horses with a bucket of food. Maureen and Sophie arrived after the other humans and Joe and me both whickered in greeting. We ate our food as the girls quietly moved about, removing our night rugs and brushing the shavings gently from our legs and belly. Munchkin neighed and scurried the length of the big stable to get his head into the food bucket before Tom could get near. Sophie laughed and pointed over to the end stable where Tom had his head in the same bucket as Munchkin. Maureen smiled. As Sophie ran her hand down my front leg and touched the inside of it, I jumped. Sophie stepped back quickly and frowned.

"What's up Malé? I'm sorry, did I hurt you?" she soothed and slowly touched all around that part of my leg until she came to the bit where I jumped again. She held my head and very lightly passed her hand over a small patch where the skin was warm and a little bit raised.

"Maureen," Sophie called through the wooden stable partition as Joe was being brushed and checked over too. "Come and have a look at this, would you? Malé's got a bit of a bump. It's a bit tender."

"Oh, now what?" Maureen quickly slips into my stable and bends over to look where Sophie points. Maureen passes her hand over the sore patch. "There's a bit of heat in it… we'd best let Fiona know before I put anything on it. Not really raised up much but…. We'd better check."

Sophie nods and goes to the end of the stable block and calls Fiona. She is back in a few moments. "She's on her way now," she tells Maureen, and picks up the bag with my brushes in and hangs it outside while Maureen checks the rest of my legs.

"It's just on the one front leg…nothing on the others. Maybe a knock or something. Let's see what Fiona has to say. He might be out for this one." She patted my neck. "No galloping about for you today, Malé, old boy, if I'm not much mistaken."

Fiona arrived, striding through the stable block to my stable, her blond hair roughly pulled into a short pony tail at the back of her head. She looked concerned. She paused as she entered my stable. "Hello Malé, my lovely. What is it then? What have you gone and done, sweetie?" Maureen pulled a face and Sophie, who stifled a giggle, told Fiona she had just found the sore patch this morning. Nothing last night.

"OK, and did he catch it on anything, do you know? All steady in the lorry?"

"Yes, as far as I know."

"OK, well, there doesn't seem to be any swelling, and the skin's not broken. Maureen can you put some of your best potion on it and walk him around for half an hour, then we'll check again. If it's still not right, we'll have to pull him for this one. Shame as we've only a couple left this season and he was about half way up the table, but still, can't have you galloping round with a sore leg, can we, eh?" she kissed my face and offered me a sweet. Joe kicked his door and stretched towards us. "Oh, Joe" she said, "you don't miss a thing do you?" and she handed Sophie the roll of mints and she gave Joe his.

Maureen put my headcollar on and Sophie got Joe and we walked out of the block together, up the gravel track and along the hedge where it was quiet. Fiona followed as far as the stable block, watching as we walked. "He doesn't seem to be lame. I'll go and get changed and meet you here in half an hour, OK?"

The girls nodded. We walked on together.

"Does it hurt?" Joe asked.

"No. Only if the humans touch it."

"How did you do it?"

"I think it was when I got my leg stuck in my bucket."

"Oh, Malé!" Joe said, and pretended to bite my neck.

***

Since I was not allowed to finish my work at the show, I was walked around with Joe while we waited for him to do his work. Sophie and Joe warmed up as Fiona watched.

"That bend in the woods is quite tight, so make sure you're steady there," she advised Sophie, "and the brush fence coming out is a big one. After that you can gallop on till you come over the hill to the ditches. Sit tight for the coffin, and try to get him back on his hocks and steady well before then." Sophie nodded and smiled. "And enjoy yourself! It's a lovely day out there, and the going is nice and firm."

Maureen held my head firmly, or I would have galloped after Joe as he set off with Sophie over the fixed jumps. Joe reassured me: "I'll be back before you know it, Malé. I'll be sure to gallop as fast as I can too." I shook my head and snorted as Joe went through the gate towards the start ready for his turn. Maureen waited until Joe was out of sight, safely over the first fence which was made out of enormous tyres with bushes over the top. Then Maureen led me to the place where the course ended to wait for Joe. I wanted to trot, keen to see Joe again, but Maureen kept hold of my rope and talked quietly to me as we made our way across the roughly mown fields.

At the end we waited behind the ropes as the horses cantered briskly past the timer who nodded as each rider went by. When Joe arrived, I neighed to greet him as soon as I saw him and he whinnied back, white sweat on his neck and belly, legs slick with water from the jumps at the bottom of the slope. Sophie sat back quietly as Joe, realizing his work was finished, slowed to a walk and stretched out his neck.

"Thank god you're back in one piece, Soph, Malé's been pining for him since we lost sight of you after the first."

"Poor old Malé," she said, "we're back now." And she jumped lightly to the ground and loosened Joe's girth and ran the stirrups up the leathers so they didn't move about. Then she loosened his noseband and Joe stretched his neck and rubbed his face on his front leg. Still panting we fell into step, heading back to the stables so Joe could have a drink and get his cooler rug on. The veins on his neck stood out and his red coat shone.

"All OK Sophie?" Fiona arrived to check everything was OK. "I saw you from the third to just after the water. I think you came in under the time, so you'll have dropped a few points there, but the going's so good everyone seems to be the same. How was it?"

"Oh, Joe was marvellous," Sophie said, still breathing hard as she removed her hard hat and unzipped her body protector. "I let him set the pace most of the way round, and it was easier to set him up than the last few outings, so yes... all good I think."

"That's progress then. And a good sign for when we move up the levels next season. They get a lot more technical at Intermediate, and you'll need all the control you can get, on top of the speed. Well, you go and get yourself sorted and we'll see you for something to eat in 15 minutes, OK?"

Maureen had already taken Joe's saddle and breastplate off and swapped his bridle for a headcollar then she threw his cooler rug over him. Fiona smiled and patted Joe and me then she gave both of us a sweet, even though I had not done any work. Then we were put back in our cages with some fresh hay until it was time for the show jumping to begin. I watched over Joe while he dozed and the afternoon sun warmed up the barn. Some flies hurried past on their way to the muck heap. A few horses stamped their feet or turned around in their stables, but mostly it was quiet. Munchkin lay with his neck curled towards his tail, his mane sticking out like an enormous hairy caterpillar and his friend Tom stood over him, eyes half closed.

I closed my eyes as Joe lay peacefully in the next stable, snoring slightly. I thought of how much I loved Joe and how terrible life would be without him by my side. But soon I fell asleep.

When the sun had started its journey back across the sky the humans began to reappear. Most of them carried saddles and bridles, in ones and twos, some smiling and laughing, some more serious. Sophie and Maureen arrived with Joe's show jumping saddle and his plain bridle with the noseband that is fitted above the bit so it is the most comfortable one that we have to wear. Sophie placed the saddle and bridle over the door of Joe's stable and went inside.

"Afternoon, Joe," she said, "time to get ready for your round. How are you feeling, now? Let's have a look at you." She ran her hands down Joe's legs and along his back, gently feeling for any problems. When she got to his shoulders she pressed Joe's muscles rhythmically, pressing harder, then softer, moving down to the top of his legs. Then around to the other side.

"Soph, what are you doing?" Maureen peered through the gaps in the wooden slats between our stables. "We're on in half an hour, you do know that?"

"I know," Sophie replied, "I'm just trying out a new massage technique. It's meant to be relaxing for them. He has been galloping round that cross country course you know."

"It won't be relaxing for anyone if we're late meeting Fiona." Maureen answered.

"She'll be fine. I'll explain it to her. It can improve performance. I'll tell her that."

Joe yawned and stretched as Sophie picked up his saddle from over the door. He seemed to have enjoyed his brief massage session.

"That's right, a good stretch and you'll be ready for anything, Joe" Sophie patted his neck gently and Joe turned to nudge her. "Those jumps are pretty huge, but we've got this, OK?"

Maureen opened my stable door and led me towards the open end of the barn where the afternoon sun made us all blink. The bright green spring grass along the edges of the path was neatly trimmed and the path sprinkled with fresh sand. The white rails shone. Everything tidy and nothing out of place. I stopped and turned to look for Joe. He had to wait while Tom was brought out of the end stable, with Munchkin by his side, bits of shavings from the bedding stuck in his big untidy mane.

"It's OK fella, Joe's on his way. Don't panic." Maureen patted my neck and we stood to the side while Tom and Munchkin passed. We fell into step with Joe as we made our way to the collecting ring.

Fiona waved and smiled when she saw us. She was dressed in her jeans and an old jacket as I was not competing that day, only Sophie and Joe. Sophie slipped out of her dark blue overalls which had covered her best jacket, white shirt and the pale jodhpurs she wore for this part of our work. Maureen took the overalls and handed Sophie her dark blue gloves. She stood at Joe's head while Sophie checked the girth was tight enough, as Joe had learnt that if you take a deep breath when it first goes on, it ends up quite loose when you breath normally again. Joe stood quietly until everything was ready.

"OK Sophie, lets go through the plan. Maureen, keep them both moving and we'll go and check out that double. I want to be sure of the distance. We can't afford more than one pole down and that's the most tricky part."

Fiona and Sophie went in the direction of the main arena where there were already lots of spectators sitting waiting for the horses to arrive to jump.

"I'll just look after these two then," Maureen mumbled as she led Joe and me away from the busiest part of the ring to where it was quietest. After we had stretched out legs a little, Maureen ran whilst we trotted along beside her for a short while.

"So Sophie, the distance means that you'll have to have Joe well collected between the first and second elements, then look....7, 8 , 9, 10... it's a little bit long, and the final spread is about as wide as you can have at this level. Bit cheeky, and it might catch a few out, so be sure to let him stretch towards that one. The last is not the biggest, but they seem to have put some kind of reflective stuff on the poles. I don't think it will bother Joe, but if the sun's in the wrong direction, you never know."

"OK." Sophie answered, nodding seriously. She looked around at all the people, their camping chairs and picnic baskets, smiling and looking forward to their afternoon's entertainment.

Fiona glanced at Sophie. "Don't worry about the crowd. The organisers are quite strict here. Dogs have to be under control, or they're out. They had an incident last year where a horse was bitten and it caught the tendon. It got infected and the horse never competed again. They're really careful now. No-one wants a repeat of that!"

"Well, that's a good thing, at least."

"Yes, and if I see anything I think is suspicious I'll be straight over to the stewards. We haven't come this far for something silly to spoil it"

"No. Thanks. I've been doing a course. Online…" Sophie's voice tailed off.

"Oh, what about?" Fiona asked, glancing at the course layout sheet in her hand.

"Equine sports massage for owners. They teach you some basic ways to help the horses relax after strenuous activity. It seems to help them. Not that I'm an owner of course," she added quickly.

Fiona smiled. "That sounds just like you Sophie. Always wanting the best for your charges. Why don't you have a try with Joe? See how he responds?"

"I will. And it might help Malé chill out a bit more, and that's got to be a good thing."

"You're right. Yes. Give it a go and let me know."

Sophie beamed as she re-joined Maureen and took Joe from her. "We're good to go. I can try the massage on them both!"

"Fantastic," Maureen replied, "and if she ever wants a hot tub I'm going in before they do!"

Sophie looked up from Joe's girth and laughed so hard she rested her head on the saddle for a moment. She wiped her eyes as she sat on Joe's back. "You do make me laugh, Maur," she said. "I can just picture them in there, glass in hoof, nibbling a few oats."

"We'd have to ban hay though, that would mess up the filters, for definite."

"Stop, it! I'm on in ten minutes."

"Go on, you'll need to pop that jump a couple of times and there's a queue."

Sophie trotted Joe off towards the edge of the collecting ring where fewer riders and horses were warming up. Sophie let Joe trot and canter quietly with his head out in front, and when it was their turn, they cleared the small fence in the middle, then the larger one at the other side. Then it was time for me to leave and wait beside the arena for Joe to finish his round. Sophie sat quietly, nodding to a few of the other riders she had seen at other events before.

"Pssst!!" a voice came from behind the rope fence near to where Joe and Sophie stood. Sophie turned in the saddle. "Tig! How did you get here?"

"I wasn't needed at the meet today and it's my day off tomorrow, and my mate Charlie offered me a lift to his nan's. She's a couple of miles up the road so I got the bus over. How's the ginger winner today?" He patted Joe's neck and ruffled his ears. Joe blew softly into Tig's hand. "No sweets, old boy, not till you've been in and done your stuff. Then there might be a mint or two. We can't be spoiling you now can we, eh?" Joe tossed his head and snorted. The announcer same something over the tannoy. "What number did he say Tig? If it was twelve I'm on next!"

"I think it was, you know. Better get off to the ringside and check. You'll both need all your concentration for that combination. That last jump's nearly five foot spread you know."

"I know. Fiona's been over it with me. We had a walk round earlier."

"Now why doesn't that surprise me?" Tig smiled and squeezed Sophie's calf underneath her shiny black boots, then he ducked back under the rope and disappeared into the crowd to find a spot and watch their round.

"Come on Joey boy. It's just you and me now. Let's go and show them what we can do." Sophie leaned forward to pat Joe's neck and then she shortened the reins and they trotted over to the arena entrance, just as the previous rider knocked down a pole at the last.

I waited with Maureen at my head. We walked around for a bit then we fell into step with the horse and rider we had met at Field Farm. The horse was grey with a heavier neck than me or Joe and powerful muscular hindquarters. His nose was slightly roman and he held his head higher in the air than most of the horses around. As his rider and Maureen chatted about the weather and the show and which of the tents sold the best food, I asked the horse why he held his head high up like that.

"Why?" he said, "I scarcely know any more. It could be the bit in my mouth and the noseband which is always so tight. Or it could be because I have not

161

had anything to eat for too long and my stomach hurts. But then, it hurts all the time now."

"But why do your humans not take care of you properly?" I asked him. "Do they not know how you hurt?"

"I don't know why. I have been living with these humans since I was ready to be a ridden horse. My first family never strapped my mouth closed like this. They were kind and I was always with my mother and brothers and sisters. They did things slowly so I could understand what I needed to do. These humans are impatient and want me to do everything right every time. I am just a horse. I can't speak their language."

The horse looked so unhappy and uncomfortable, I wished I could help him. He took a step back and his rider jerked the reins so the horse threw his head a little higher. I remembered how the bit had hurt my mouth when Fiona had had her fall. I stretched out my neck to touch him gently and he dared not move in case the bit hurt his mouth again.

It was soon time to go and meet Joe after his showjumping round. Maureen said goodbye to the rider and he dug his heels into the horse's sides and he trotted briskly away from us. I watched him go and hoped that his humans would take better care of him.

Sophie and Joe had already finished their round when we found them in the collecting ring. Tig was holding Joe whilst Sophie undid the girth and she was smiling happily. Fiona arrived to join us.

"Well, I don't know how, but you managed to pull that one off this time!" Fiona exclaimed.

"It's a good job Joe tucked his feet up at the combination. He was going like a train," Tig said.

"You were so close on landing, Sophie, but they all stayed up. Well done!" Fiona beamed.

"Yes, I knew we were coming in too fast, but Joe seemed really up for it, and he can shorten up really well if he needs to, so I thought we'd just go for it. And he did really well!"

"Wow. You're two seconds quicker than the next fastest. And only three to go!" Maureen squeaked. I whinnied at Joe, just glad we were back together again. He nuzzled my neck, sides still heaving after the effort of his round.

"Better keep him moving, we don't want him getting stiff. Here, Tig, take Joe for a stroll while Sophie gets a drink will you?" Tig hugged Sophie's shoulders and then took Joe's reins. We walked around slowly together until Joe's breathing was back to normal and he had stopped sweating. The breeze was cool as the sun was now low in the sky and Maureen said we should put Joe's rug over his quarters. Tig reached into the horse box for Joe's rug as we passed and threw it on with one flick of his hand. Joe twisted his neck and pulled at the hay net tied to the outside. He looked quite tired now with his head low and one leg resting behind. Maureen handed my lead rope to Tig and got us both some water. Joe gulped down half the bucket and went back to his hay. Fiona and Sophie arrived with another rosette.

"Right folks, home time. Do you want dropping off anywhere Tig, or are you in the box with the girls?" Fiona asked.

"Oh, if it's OK Mrs Weston, I'd like a lift back in the box. My friend who gave me a lift down here is staying the night with his nan. It's her birthday you see, and she's 90, so I expect he'd be too tipsy to ride back."

"I bet his nan will drink him under the table," Fiona answered. "You're welcome to a lift. I'll see you back at the yard. Take your time, and well done everybody!" She turned to head back to the car park for the journey home.

Sophie tied the rosette alongside the last one, then she took it off, moved some of them along and put her latest one right in the middle. Then she knelt on the seat and smiled.

Many Questions

After that show Joe and me were allowed out in the field with the retired geldings for some time to relax before the last shows of the season. Joe and me galloped around for a while when we were first turned out, breathing in lungfuls of fresh spring air, before we noticed the bright green grass and dropped our heads to eat, grasping each mouthful with our teeth and snatching it, stepping slowly forwards to the next, and the next, until our stomachs were full and it was time for a snooze beside the hedge where it was sheltered from the wind as it blew across the valley.

One of us usually kept watch while the other slept, but here, with the two other horses whose field we shared, we could both lie down and sleep at the same time as they watched. Joe slept with his body stretched out, whilst I lay curled close by, my waterproof rug keeping the breeze from my closely clipped skin. I awoke first, as a group of crows squabbled over their favourite branches of the chestnut tree. I watched as they flew from treetop to treetop, squarking and flapping, finally flying off towards the open fields beyond their woods.

Joe sat up, yawned and stretched his long neck, then pulled himself up by his front legs and shook himself all over.

"Wake up lazy bones," he said, shoving my hind quarters with his nose. I stood up and followed him slowly down to the water trough. After we had drunk our fill we went back to where Quest and Finn were waiting. They lay beside us, closed their eyes and were soon fast asleep.

"It's so much nicer than being in our cages all the time, out here, with the grass and the breeze."

Joe agreed. "I like to have a good roll in the damp grass, that always makes me feel better, especially if my shoulders are stiff after a long journey."

"Yes. It's very hard to do that in our cages. Not nearly enough room."

We watched as a tractor rumbled along the road and turned off onto the track up to the farm opposite. There were no horses there, only some cows and sometimes a few sheep.

"Joe?" I asked. "You know when you did your jumping on your own when I hurt my leg and it swelled up a bit?"

"Yes. What about it?" Joe answered.

"Well, we were waiting for you to finish your jumping, and Maureen was speaking to the rider of that horse we saw at Field Farm. He was so uncomfortable. He said that the noseband was so tight, and the bit hurt his mouth, and that his stomach hurt all the time."

"Oh," said Joe. "That's not good. Did he tell you why his stomach hurt?"

"No, he didn't know. But he said he didn't get to eat for a long time so at first it hurt just sometimes, but now it hurts all the time."

Quest lifted his head: "Horses need to eat little and often. When we don't our stomachs hurt." Then he went back to sleep. Finn sighed deeply. "He's right,

166

we need to have something in our stomachs. It happens to lots of horse who work hard and don't get to eat for hours."

"So, lots of the horses we meet at shows, and the racehorses we live with, do their stomachs hurt too?" I asked.

"Yes." Finn replied. "The humans are different. They are more like dogs. They can go for a longer time without eating and it doesn't hurt them at all. Although they can get grumpy. But not like horses. We have to eat, and when our work takes us away from food, well, our stomachs just don't cope very well after a while."

"Did your stomach hurt, when you were racing?"

"Oh yes," said Finn. "But now we are retired, it hardly hurts at all any more."

"Doesn't yours hurt Malé?" Joe asked.

"Sometimes. When you went to another yard I couldn't eat properly, and it did then. And when my mouth got hurt too. How about you, Joe?"

"Well, it did sometimes when I was in race training. But when we are out working I always try to snack on the grass or the hedges when the humans aren't looking. To keep my stomach topped up."

"That is a very good idea, Joe," said Finn.

"I'm going to try that too." A cloud passed over the sun and a soft breeze made the new leaves whisper to each other. "Another thing I have seen, which I don't understand is why lots of the humans carry whips with them and use them to hurt their horses. Why do they do that? The horses never did them any harm."

167

"Well Malé," Finn explained, "there is a thing called winning. The humans want very much to win. Sometimes so much they forget that horses are meant to be their friends."

"But why does winning mean they have to be cruel?"

"The jockeys mostly had whips at the races," Joe said, "and sometimes they hit their horses with them. But I don't know why."

"It is because they think it makes us run faster. And when we run faster, they win. That's what I was saying. Winning is what matters."

"It's not very fair, I mean, hitting someone. It doesn't make me run faster."

"No Malé," said Joe, "but we are eventers, so galloping fast isn't what it takes to win. We have to do dressage and bend nicely and all that stuff. And when we are jumping at the end, well, if we went too fast, we would just fall over. And then we wouldn't ever win anything."

"So the riders at the shows we go to shouldn't need a whip at all!"

"Fiona carries a whip. She sometimes taps you with it. On your belly."

"Yes, she does, but it really doesn't hurt. In fact, it just tickles mostly."

"What you need to understand," said Finn, "is that humans cannot hear us speaking. We have to learn what they want in their language. And quite often, they are not clear and we have to work it out. They find it frustrating sometimes."

168

I remembered when we first did our lessons in the little yard when Joe and I were just yearlings. Sophie and Maureen were always kind and gentle and what we had to do was easy so we learnt fast. And they never carried a whip. I am quite sure Fiona would not have allowed anyone to hit us, or to hurt our mouths with rough hands.

"I am not sure about Sophie though. I think she can speak our language sometimes."

"I know what you mean, Malé," answered Joe, "sometimes I tell her things and I think she does understand."

"How so?" asked Finn.

Joe thought for a moment. "Well, when we are working, and she is not on my back, I sometimes forget she is just a human, and not a horse, as she knows what I am saying when I move in a certain way, or by the look in my eye if I am not happy about something. If I get confused, she changes what she is doing so I understand better. She always notices things."

"She is a very unusual human," Finn said. "Perhaps some of those who find it acceptable to hit horses should learn from her."

"Yes! They should!" we all agreed.

"And why must we always be put back in our cages, and have our fur clipped away, and metal on our feet? All these things which we would never choose, if we ever had the choice."

"So many questions, Malé. I think they are done to help us do our very best to win."

169

"Oh, that again! Perhaps the humans should run in races and jump over things themselves and then they could win all day long and horses would not have to do all these things for them."

"Oh, they do," said Finn, "but some humans are not strong enough or fast enough, so they choose horses as their way to win."

"And what happens to horses who don't win? Where do they end up?"

There was a silence as Quest stood up, yawning. He heaved a big sigh and said that many are sold to other people who don't need to win so much, but some are sent on lorries and no-one ever sees them again.

"Did you win, when you were racehorses?" Joe asked Finn and Quest.

"Yes. Sometimes. At least, I think so. I ran in flat races, where there are no big hedges to jump, and Finn did the ones with big jumps. They are generally longer races and you just have to keep on galloping and jumping. The flat races, you have to be quick to start, out of the gates, and run like the wind until you hear the people at the other end cheering, and then you can slow down."

"That sounds like very hard work."

"It is," said Joe, "and although the jockeys are not so heavy, sometimes it hurts your back, to run so fast and not slow down."

"Yes. And the races get longer as you get a bit older, you know."

"Oh," said Joe, "I wasn't a racehorse for very long. Then I became an eventer with Malé. We go everywhere together you know. All our training, every show, we travel side by side and even ride out into the woods together when we are at home."

"It is nice to have friends. You two have each other and Finn and me do too."

"Have you always been together, like us?"

"No. We come from different stables. But I think we have the same owner. The same human comes to see us both sometimes. Quest and me. We were born on different farms, but now our work is finished, we stay here together all the time."

"I hope Joe and me are together always. We were born here, and apart from when Joe was taken away, we've been best friends since we were just foals." Memories of my mother flooded back, the mare who cared for me when I was orphaned, and of when I first met Joe, of Magic and wonderful Ace and the field where we grew up together until we were separated from our mothers and never saw them again.

"Come on, let's go and try the grass down by the stream, we might find some different plants there for a change." Joe always knows when it is time to stop thinking.

We ran ahead tossing our heads and kicking up our heels as we cantered down the slope to the stream. Quest and Finn followed behind, knowing there was always plenty of grass to go around, and there was no need to rush. Their days of rushing and of winning were over. Now it was time for peace.

A Change of Heart

There were only a few more shows that year, and then it was time for our late summer holidays. The man with the metal tools came by to take off our shoes and trim our hooves. Usually, he put a fresh set back on again, driving long nails into the horn of our feet to fix the shoes on tight, so this time, when there were no new shoes, we knew it was different. When we have no shoes fixed on our feet it takes a while for the blood to flow back into them, and they tingle for a few days, and stepping on a stone can feel quite sharp, but the next morning we had our feed and a brush down, and instead of our saddles and bridles being put on, Maureen and Sophie just put on our headcollars and clipped a short rope to the ring.

"Here we go then. Holiday time for you boys!" Maureen swung the stable door wide open and Joe and me were taken to the lorry where we carefully walked up the ramp and were tied there side by side.

"Soph! Soph! Are you ready? We've got to get back sometime today you know. Those horses can't have dirty stables."

Sophie came out from the tea room pulling on her short coat.

"Give me a minute. It's all that tea you've made this morning."

"I dunno why you can't just go behind a bush like the rest of us. Call yourself a stable hand? Pfftttt!"

Maureen climbed into the driver's seat of the horse box and Sophie ran to open the gate. She only just got it open as Maureen drove through and stopped the other side until it was firmly shut and bolted and Sophie was beside her in the passenger seat.

"What's the rush? Have you got an extra half day off you haven't told me about?"

"Oh, no rush. I was just saying that for the jockeys to hear. I want to pop in to that new coffee shop in Alverton. They do the most incredible cakes, apparently."

"Yes, I heard that too. Carrot cake and lemon meringue pie. All that old fashioned stuff."

"But you can't have any, sadly. You need to stay thin. For Joe's sake."

"Joe's having a holiday and won't get ridden for 3 weeks, so I can eat as many cakes as I like. In fact, I might have two!"

"Oooh look at you, pushing the boat out. You won the lottery or something?"

"No, it's the grooms prize. We got nearly £200 each."

"I know. The cakes are on you!"

"OK, just this once. But I'm saving up to go on a course."

"Oh god, not one of those tree huggers courses? Not again Soph, I mean, how long it take to learn how to hug a tree?"

"Three days this time. A long weekend."

"Do they feed you and everything?"

"Oh yes. Three meals a day and snacks in between with vegetarian and vegan options available, if you're interested."

"I'm not," Maureen answered firmly. She swung the lorry into a small yard and stopped the engine. "Right, let's get these two turned out and settled, then next stop Alverton."

Sophie closed the gate while Maureen unbolted the big door at the back of the lorry to let us out. Joe whinnied when he saw Sophie and she patted his neck gently as she unclipped him and led him down to the yard. Maureen and me followed, and we were taken down a short sandy track into a big field with high hedges and a row of trees across the middle. There was an open barn which had rusty panels and the light came in through holes in the roof, sending beams of sunlight to the hard packed ground illuminating the fine dust that hung in the air.

"Off you go boys, and behave yourselves. We'll be back tomorrow."

We were taken through the gate and turned towards it. The ropes were unclipped and we spun round and galloped away, me in front and Joe close behind. The summer field! Days of wandering about, eating, drinking, sleeping, rolling and doing everything we loved to do whenever we wanted for three whole weeks! No metal shoes, no rugs, no cages and no work!

"They look happy," Sophie said as she and Maureen strolled back along the track to the horse box.

"They sure do. I hope they'll come back fresh and ready to get back into training. Fiona's got big plans for them this year."

"I know. Intermediate. I'd better start learning the dressage tests already."

"Don't worry I'll read it out to you until Joe's got it. He can be the brains of the operation."

"And I'll have to work on medium trot as opposed to working trot."

"Fiona will have to explain that one again. I'm not sure I can tell myself, to be honest."

"I've read the instructions over and over, but I can't say it's clear once I'm riding."

"There must be some videos or something," Maureen mused as she slammed the horse box door closed and fiddled with her seat belt.

"I expect so."

"Then there's half pass, and that shoulder in thing, and a lot of turns."

"Yes."

"I think Malé prefers the galloping about thing. And the show jumping."

"I thought you liked dressage?"

"I used to, but only because it was less likely that I'd get ditched and fall off in front of everyone, even if Penny wouldn't bend properly in the corners and always edged back to the entrance."

"No chance of any medium trot then?"

"No such refinements. Did you see the programme we bought at that event? Their dressage horse had no tack at all."

"That's where you went wrong then. Putting a saddle and bridle on."

"I saw a lovely bareback saddle pad, you know. At the last show. Purple suede, it was."

"Ew. Tack should be brown. Always. And how can it be bareback if it's a kind of saddle?"

"It's just padded to protect their spine. You can feel their movements better."

"Can't see Fiona letting you get that on Joe."

"No." Sophie looked thoughtful.

After a short drive through the lanes Maureen pulled the horse box into a car park by the village green and turned the key. "Come on, cakes and cappuchino here we come!"

A bell rang as Maureen opened the wooden front door of the tiny shop. The owner greeted them with a smile, wiping her hands on her apron.

"What can I get for you?" she said.

"OOhhh, I don't know. There's such a lot to choose from…" Maureen bent to get a proper view of all the cakes at the back of the counter. "Is that lemon drizzle?" she asked, pointing to the one right at the back.

"Yes, but we do orange as well. Just here." She pointed out the cake nearest to Maureen under a glass cover.

"I tell you what, can I have a small piece of each please?"

"What all of them?" Sophie said.

"No, silly, just the lemon and orange drizzle. I can't decide."

"Of course." The café owner answered, smiling again. "We get asked that a lot. We were thinking of doing a sort of platter of really small ones, so people can try a few, and then hopefully take a whole one home with them."

"You do takeaway?"

"Yes. But only the full ones, or a single full sized piece." Maureen stared, open mouthed.

"I'll have the pineapple one please. And a large tea," Sophie got her purse from her bag and got out her bank card. "These are on me!"

"Oooh thanks. I might have seconds then," Maureen looked back at the counter longingly.

"You won't! You're already having two."

"Two small ones. Not the full thing," Maureen protested, mildly.

"Shall we pick the best one and take a whole one back to the yard?"

"Not this time, or they'll know we skived off when we were supposed to be supervising the event horses' holidays."

"I'm sure they'd be prepared to keep our secret, in exchange for a piece of that chocolate cake."

"Nah. They're jockeys. They're always on a diet."

"More for us then!" Sophie laughed and took her white mug full of steaming tea to the nearest table. Maureen followed and they waited for their cakes to arrive. A rare treat. They savoured each mouthful, smiling and joking about their crazy lives, scraping the last crumbs from their plates with the tiny silver forks.

Maureen sat back, putting her hand on her stomach. "Phew. That was amazing. We should do this more often. We hardly ever get out."

"We've been to eighteen shows this year!"

"Yes, but that's work. Time off is precious. More cake is a definite bonus, specially after eating all those rank hot dogs from vans."

"I thought you liked them?"

"Not really, but what else is there? Food's really expensive at those places and hot dogs are the cheapest. That's all. You'd think Fiona would keep an eye on what you eat."

"Me? Why? I'm not a bit fat. Yet."

"You're as thin as a pin, love. Turn sideways and you could hide behind a schooling whip. I meant with you being an athlete now. Riding her second best event horse. Would've thought she'd have had you on some kind of vitamins by now."

"The horses are fed better than us. Did you see than new powder they're both on? Over £50 a bag."

"You could always slip yourself a teaspoon of that."

"No thanks."

"Seriously though, Soph, you should look after yourself. You could have a great career on the back of this."

Sophie gazed out of the window for moment. "Not sure I'd want that," she replied, gazing into her half empty mug and fiddling with her crumpled serviette.

"Why not?" Maureen frowned at her friend. "even if it's not here, you're bound to get offered a ride elsewhere. And get more money, if they have a half decent sponsor."

"Definitely not if that's the case. It's all about winning then. The horses suffer."

"Suffer? Of course they don't suffer. Those event horses are pampered all day long."

"And they have to have their hocks injected with steroids half way through the season. And some of them are buted up so they can carry on training. I'm OK with Fiona, the way she does it. But not those big commercial yards. I couldn't hack that."

"So… what would you do instead? Joe and Malé will have to retire at some point. They don't last long at the top level."

"Exactly. I've thought about it a lot and I reckon this barefoot bunny hugging thing, as you call it, is the way forward. I think more people want to be sure their horses are happy, rather than just winning rosettes. There's got to be a way to help those sort of people."

"So it's not just the latest fad? Like fancy nosebands and hacking out with draw reins?"

"Maybe. Don't you think horses deserve to be happy? And not pushed to their limits all the time?"

"I don't think they'd know any difference really. Horses have always been worked. It was a lot worse when they pulled carts. Then it was a family's livelihood."

"Then, yes. But it's not the same now. There's cars."

"So horses should just be pets? Is that what you mean?"

"No, of course not."

"Cos if they were, we'd be out of a job straightaway."

"I know, but there's got to be a kinder way. One where the horses get a say and we can still enjoy being around them."

"God, you're weird!" Maureen got up and pulled the keys out of her pocket. "Come on, it's time we got back, Miss Jones. Stables won't muck themselves out." Sophie smiled at her friend and they left the tea shop arm-in-arm.

***

"It is thought that metal horseshoes, the nailed on kind were first used around five or six hundred AD. And the design has changed very little since then, although the metal would have been re-worked and made into other things once the shoes were worn, so there's not enough evidence to really tell what the details were.

"Cast bronze horseshoes were common in just about the whole of Europe by about 1000AD. Fast forward to 1800, to the work of Bracy Clark, who observed the changes in the horse's hooves after long periods of shoeing. He worked at the London Veterinary College, and produced a whole range of drawings showing how the hoof contracts with repeated shoeing.

"DVW Zerold did a study in 1910 and found that a shod hoof experiences three times the impact when trotting on a hard surface, compared to one without, and also that the metal in a shoe vibrates at 800 hertz, which damages living tissue. So, we see that the idea of protecting a horse's hooves by nailing metal to them is a bit of myth. It just doesn't stand up to the evidence. There's a lot more research being done now, and I'll give you a list at the end if you want to read up on it."

Sophie stared at the screen, open-mouthed, her pen dangling from her hand.

"Amazing isn't it?" a whisper from the next seat along. "I never knew any of this."

"Yes. No, I mean, it's pretty shocking."

"I'm looking forward to hearing how we go about getting rid of them, so I can sort mine out when I get home."

Sophie turned to her colleague and smiled. "That's great. I don't have my own horses and I doubt my employer would allow hers to go without shoes. So I'll have to save it for another time."

"Do you work for a riding school?"

"No, a racing yard. But I also ride my employer's event horse, Joe, he's a sweetie."

"Oh, you event. That's amazing. I did hear there's a racing yard that keeps the horses barefoot. They last longer then, and they have less lameness."

"That will only catch on if they run faster" Sophie answered, turning back to the screen as the teacher continued.

"Although some remnants of what we might call 'hoof boots' have also been found, also mainly in

182

Europe, they were gradually replaced by metal shoes. The hoof boots were made of leather, with straps holding them around the horse's fetlock. Here you can see what has been called the 'hipposandal', it's quite padded, so it's unlikely to have caused the amount of damage to a horse's hooves that a metal shoe does, and of course, they can be adjusted and taken off completely."

"So, what can we conclude from this? Do we all need to go home and get our horse's shoes removed immediately? Well, that would be nice, but before we do, it's good to have a plan and to be realistic to give it the best chance of success. The last thing you'd want is for your horse to transition to being barefoot, then be forced to go back to having metal shoes nailed on again, and it can be quite heart-breaking for us as owners too. It's quite a roller-coaster and definitely not for the faint-hearted."

"Well if it's best for the horses, I'm all for it," Sophie's new friend said firmly. Sophie smiled, then she turned to her notebook and sighed.

There was a knock at the open classroom door and a trolley arrived, laden with the first snacks of the day. Silver coloured jugs with sticky labels on the top, tea, coffee, hot water, and individual packets of biscuits in a small wicker basket. Tiny bags of peanuts and an oval plate of fresh fruit. The teacher lifted a cardboard box from the floor and placed it on the desk in readiness for the next session while everyone gathered around the trolley. She lifted out some models: several hooves, a front leg, a back leg, cut away to show the structures inside, and a large rolled up image of the horse's musculature, each muscle and tendon carefully labelled in tiny writing. She pinned it to the whiteboard at the front with some blobs of Blutack and set about straightening it.

Sophie caught one end of it as it flopped down from the wall. "Here, let me help," she dragged a chair and stood on it then added some more Blutack to the top corner and pressed hard so the picture stayed up. "That should do it." The teacher smiled and thanked her.

"How are you finding it so far?" she asked.

"Oh, it's amazing stuff. Most of it is new to me. Horse have always been shod wherever I've been."

"I'm not surprised, it's a fact of life. People are just trying to do the best for their horses, and most of the time they cope, but when it goes wrong, the consequences for the horses are enormous."

"Yes, I see a lot of that. With the racehorses. Coming off the track there are lots of problems."

"Ah, racing. There's another tale. It's not just shoes for them. They're in work way too young, before their bodies are mature. We're going to look at that next. I hope you'll find it interesting. It can seem a bit dry, so that's why I keep it short and do this one before lunch."

"I'm sure I will," Sophie replied. "We learn the basics at college, but after that, it's really up to us. And I'm hired for my practical skills, that's all."

"So, your employer hasn't sent you?"

"Oh no. That would never happen! I paid for it myself. I'm all for new ideas. To make life better for the horses."

"Good for you. We must keep in touch. Are you on the mailing list?"

"I think so. I'll check."

Sophie returned to her seat with her coffee and looked over her notes. Not much to show for half a morning's work. She hoped the handouts would remind her of everything, especially all those muscles and tendons.

"OK everybody, let's move on to the next subject, and I hope you've all topped up on coffee, as this is the most detailed anatomy we're going to cover today. It's all in the notes, and the most important parts are really quite simple, so don't worry."

The next hour flew by, as the teacher explained briefly how the jaw and tongue affect movement even in the hind legs due to the tendon attachments running throughout the body. The models were passed around and discussions were had as the students pored over them, pointing and prodding, sharing stories of horses they'd met who needed their owners to understand all this. One of the girls in Sophie's group said she'd been to a whole horse dissection and they'd been shown how to pull the tendon in the jaw so the hindleg moved.

"Really?" the girl next to Sophie questioned.

"Oh yes. It was quite freaky. Someone actually screamed." Everyone laughed.

"I'm not surprised," Sophie said, "I've only ever seen a dead horse twice, and neither time it was pleasant."

"Wow. What happened?"

"One was a car accident, the other a gelding operation that got infected."

"That's really sad."

"So, who keeps their horses barefoot?"

"One of mine's never had shoes. She's a welshie. Bit of a madam. Doubt any farrier would want to try getting shoes on her anyway!"

"I don't have my own, so…"

"You never know. When you do get your own, you can do what you like."

"Yes. I think it must be best for the horses. In the long run."

"Two of mine are, and they do OK, but my friend has one that does all sorts. Dressage, jumping, all kinds of stuff."

"I thought you couldn't do dressage barefoot?"

"Would they even notice?"

"You mean bitless. You can't compete in dressage bitless."

"True, not at the higher levels."

"Oh really?" Sophie said. "Why is that? I would have thought they'd move better."

"They do, but it's the training of them. No-one knows how without gadgets."

"I've seen it done, at an event in Chepstow."

"Oh! Was it Josh Bygraves? I wanted to go there but it was quite expensive. He has that rehab place in the States."

"Yes, him. It was awesome. I was at a race meeting nearby. Just got lucky with the timing."

"There's a couple in the UK too though. They send really poorly horses there and they come back after six months like new."

"That would be Brickyard Farm," the teacher joined them. "They have a great setup there. All kinds of surfaces and loads of space. The horses all come right in the end. Not much they can't fix down there."

"And they don't use shoes or anything?"

"Not at all. In fact, the horses are often written off by the time they get there after their owners have tried everything, all the shoes going. So they have nothing to lose by that stage. Brickyard Farm only use natural methods, lots of turnout and remedial trims, but no shoes."

"And no operations?"

"No operations either. Horses can heal themselves, if we set it up for them. So, how did you get on with filling in the diagram?"

"Errmmmmm…"

"Don't worry, here's the answers," she smiled and handed out some papers. "Swap with the next group, I think yours is the hind leg next."

"That's amazing. I've heard about Brickyard Farm. My friend would have tried getting her horse in there after a tendon injury if only she'd known."

"What happened in the end? Did the horse recover?"

"No, she had loads of vets try, same with farriers, but she drew the line at operations, so he was retired. They said he would never compete again, but I think he does a bit of hacking here and there."

"That's heart-breaking. When they get ill."

"Yes, especially when it's humans that have made it happen."

Another student opened her mouth to speak, but the teacher asked everyone to stop and share their answers and comment on what they had learnt.

There were lots of new words, names of tendons and muscles, which bits joined onto the next. By lunchtime Sophie's head was reeling.

"Phew! That was hard work. I'm sure I'll never remember the names of everything."

Sophie nodded. "I think I'll save all these drawings though. As a reference for when I'm speaking to vets and the like. Make me sound like I know what I'm on about."

"Good idea. What did you pick for lunch?"

"Lasagne. You?"

"Veggie pizza and green salad. If it's horrible we could swap?"

"It better not be. I'm starving."

The food was brought in and the doors to the outdoor paved area opened. It was a fine day, if a little cool, and most people wandered out with their food and sat on the plastic chairs. It was pleasant out of the breeze.

"How's the lasagne?" Sophie's new friend asked.

"Really good. Lots of vegetables. And plenty of cheese on the top. How's the pizza?"

"Yes, lovely. It's a bit more practical this afternoon. We get to meet the horses."

"I know. I can't wait. Proper barefoot horses!" Sophie gazed across towards the stables. She stopped, fork half way to her mouth, staring at a tall black horse in the end stable. She frowned. "It can't be. No. It can't."

"What can't?"

"That black horse. It looks just like Reggie."

"Reggie? Are we looking at the horse?" Sophie's friend leaned over to follow her gaze.

"Yes. The black one in the end stable. It looks just like him. Can't be. He'd be what… nearly twenty-five now. But that blaze. It's exactly the same."

"Your horse?"

"No. He belonged to the riding school and livery yard owner where I used to keep Penny, my welsh pony. Was lame on and off for years and they never got to the bottom of it. Had to be retired in the end. Shame as he was a lovely boy. Taught loads of people to ride."

"Oooh it would be nice if it was him, still going strong."

"Yes. It would. Poor Reggie. The things he went through."

"Loads of different shoes, I bet."

"Yes. You name it, he had it."

"And he never came right?"

189

"No, he was just retired and one of the people who he'd taught to ride had him to keep her old mare company."

"Wonder how he ended up here then? If it is him."

"I can't wait to find out!"

"OK, everyone, let's get over to the stables for the next session. We have three horses for you to meet, all of them with a story to tell."

Plates, cups and serviettes were hurriedly shoved back on the trolley, bags grabbed, papers gathered, mobile phone pushed into pockets. Sophie and her new friend, Jill, were first over there.

"Look, it says Reggie on his stable door!" Jill exclaimed.

"Oh my! It does!" Sophie headed straight for the horse, who whinnied and tossed his head, then placed his soft brown muzzle into Sophie's hands.

The teacher caught up, smiling. "Looks like someone's got a new friend" she said as Sophie leaned over the stable door to see Reggie's leg markings.

"It's him! It's Reggie!" she turned to Jill, "I'm sure of it."

"Ah, that explains it, you already know him," the teacher said, "I wondered why he whinnied at you, he doesn't normally do that."

"I looked after him a few times when his owner was away. He was at a riding school for a long time."

"Yes he was. He came to us after he'd been retired after several years of intermittent lameness and lots of remedial interventions, which didn't help much."

Everyone stepped back as Reggie was brought out of his stable and stood quietly stretching his neck to look at everyone, checking if anyone had treats. Sophie rummaged in her jacket pocket and Reggie stepped towards her.

"Good old Reggie, he can spot a treat from a hundred metres," the teacher smiled.

"Is he allowed?" Sophie asked, keeping her hands, and the sweets in her pocket.

"Is it sugar free?"

"Yes. Definitely."

"OK, just one. And that brings us the one of the main principles in keeping a horse barefoot. Feed for the feet, and that includes strictly no sugar."

"The aim should be to provide the horse with a diet which is as close to one that a wild horse would eat as possible. That means their main source of everything has got to be forage. If they are in a field, then aim for low sugar grass, so, an old fashioned, permanent, mixed species meadow, and hay from the same, if you can get it. That means the NSC content is below twelve per cent. Of course, Reggie here was rehabilitated from suspensory ligament issues in all four feet, so he was put on a grass-free track during his first 3 months, with bare earth surfaces, then, after about a month, when his feet were better at supporting his weight, he was moved to a nearby track with a mixture of surfaces, as this stimulates the hooves to respond much more quickly, so he could trimmed more often and helped to get back to health as quickly as possible.

"No grass at all?" Jill asked.

"None at all! The sugars in grass, especially in the spring an autumn, or when it's stressed by things like over-grazing or dry weather can cause inflammation in the laminae in the hooves, which shows up as low grade laminitis and slows down hoof growth. He was fed a plain chaff with some chopped straw with his supplements, just a couple of handfuls a day, when he came in to be checked and trimmed if it was time. A good balancer is vital, and any extra vitamins to boost the quality of the horn at the same time."

"Not sure mine would eat that. They'll only eat the sweet stuff."

"Yeah, I've got a fussy eater as well."

"We do add a few small pieces of fruit and veg, apple or carrot, maybe a parsnip or swede or some fresh herbs if they like them, such as mint. When we get back to the classroom we'll look up the details of some of the feeds on the market. I think you'll be surprised."

"The issue for Reggie was that, as a heavier built horse, any imbalance will throw the whole system out massively. You might get away with a rough trim on a welsh section A for example, but with a 16.2 draft type like Reggie, a small imbalance creates a big problem."

"He used to carry heavier riders too, quite a lot," Sophie said, "sometimes he'd do five hours a day, hacking and in the school."

"Yes, so again, the added weight will compound any issue already there. Which is what happened for

Reggie. He has a natural tendency to be one sided, which isn't a problem, all horses are. People are too, we're right or left handed. The problem comes when the limbs are not properly supported by the hoof, as when they are shod, so the upper limb, from fetlock to shoulder at the front, and hocks at the back, have to move differently so the horse can balance and move without discomfort. Most of the strain was taken up by Reggie's ligaments, so he ended up constantly lame."

Reggie was trotted up and down the yard, enjoying the attention.

"Can he be ridden now?"

"Oh yes. The rehab horses are ridden when they're considered ready. Maybe not to the level they were before, simply because some damage might still be there, but their recovery is taken as far as possible at Brickyard, and they come back with a plan for keeping them well and fully functioning."

Reggie's rehab was covered in detail, his feet picked up and hooves pored over, then, after lots of strokes and another mint, he was turned out into the nearest paddock, where he trotted away happily to rejoin his friends.

Next, a grey welsh pony was brought out of her stable.

"This mare came to us after she was due to be put to sleep with founder in three hooves. The vets had tried everything they could, but in the end, they advised euthanasia as the kindest option. In fact, we had quite a struggle persuading the owner to let us try, as she'd been through so much by that stage. But luckily, one of the other vets in the practice knew what we do here and suggested letting her come over for two weeks and if there was still no improvement, then see what's best. So the owner agreed and brought her here eight months ago barely able to walk. We had to put carpets across the yard to get her into the pen. She was a very poorly pony."

"So, you didn't put her on box rest?"

"Oh no. No improvement without movement. The trick with this type of case is to allow any movement they are capable of, without forcing and causing any more damage. We put boots and 2 layers of padding at first, but took them off for half an hour every day. She was fed on some lovely old hay we reserve for animals as sick as Misty, and at first she hardly ate at all, but after a week she was able to walk confidently from one end of the pen to the other between the piles of hay. We were soon able to do tiny bits of trimming, and when the 2 weeks were up she was much happier and sound at a gentle walk in hoof boots but with no pads. Still a long way to go at that stage, but she'd done so well her owner let her stay. Look at the angle of her hooves, though. You can see the new growth, from the last eight months, compared to what she had growing when she arrived." Everyone peered at Misty's hooves, craning over each other's shoulders. Lots of oohs and ahhs when they saw it. A story told in lines and angles, nothing hidden, all there to see, if you just knew where to look.

Back to work

"Change the rein at H, medium trot, through X to F…working trot at F…collected canter right at A…." Maureen called out the instructions as Fiona rode round the arena. "Collected canter, twenty metre circle right… simple change at X… track left at E.."

When it was finished, we stood in the centre with Sophie, Maureen and Joe.

"The working trot – did you see the difference?" Fiona asked.

"I think so," Sophie answered, "it's a bit closer to extended trot, but not quite?"

"Yes, that's about it really. Stay soft and rounded, don't be tempted to push on too much, and don't forget your half halt before you ask for collected canter at A. Joe does like to run on a bit if you don't keep him steady."

"Do a full circuit to loosen him up and we'll try the trot transitions first before you go through the full test" Fiona instructed as she dismounted and handed my reins to Maureen and took the sheet of A4 paper with the test instructions printed out on it. Maureen loosened my girth, undid the strap on my noseband and ran the stirrups up the leathers, then slowly walked me around well out of Joe's way. Fiona watched Joe as he went round the edge of the arena. Sophie asked Joe to trot along the long side and touched Joe's sides gently, he increased his pace a little.

"Bit too fast, sit back a bit...leg on.. flex.... Yes! That's it. You've got him!"

Joe tossed his head and twisted his neck a little. "Hang on," Fiona said, "Bring him over a second."

Sophie halted Joe in front of Fiona and she stepped forward to put her fingers under his noseband. "Hmmmm... it's perhaps a bit tight. Let's loosen it and see if that helps. They lose a bit of momentum shaking their heads, so we want to avoid it if possible." Joe stretched his neck out and opened his mouth for a moment.

"There, walk him on a loose rein then try again with the trot, do your transition at M this time."

Sophie concentrated hard and Joe settled into his trot much better this time. Then he went through his test.

"Very good!" Fiona exclaimed, as Sophie dismounted and patted Joes neck. "Some time off has done them good. The leg yield was much more relaxed, especially on his stiffer side."

"Yes, he felt lighter somehow, so the canter transitions were much easier."

"That's the idea. Light and flowing. Coming on nicely. Now, next week we've got showjumping so could you make sure they get some long stretches of cantering. Nice and steady, nothing crazy, just to make sure their breathing is good, and we'll practice some doubles on Thursday."

And so it went on. That season was our best so far. We jumped and ran and trotted and stopped. We stayed over at many places and rested as well as we could until we were taken back to our own home. Fiona and Sophie were complimented on how well we did and Maureen was asked many questions while she waited for us to finish our work.

But near the end, something happened which changed all our lives forever.

The Fall

The day began like so many others. We were loaded onto the horse box one dark evening, and travelled to the next venue, swaying with the movement of each bend in the road as we went. Sophie and Maureen took care of us, finding our stables and ensuring we had enough food and water for the night. Then we were left until the morning.

It was a bright Autumn day and a brisk breeze made the tops of the bare trees sway a little as it passed. Joe and me watched through the open end of the large barn. As the light filtered through the high windows, the humans began to arrive. Most of them had different humans to take care of them and their riders came along later. Only Joe and a pale coloured mare had the same human for both. Joe whinnied as Sophie arrived. She spoke softly and rubbed his neck gently, then she gave him his sweet, as she always did, and took off his rug, running her hands lightly over his legs and belly, pressing his back and neck, watching his response. Then she got her bag of brushes and bandages as Maureen plonked Joe's dressage saddle over the stable door.

"You spoil that horse," she said.

"Not really," Sophie answered as she knelt at Joe's front leg, wrapping the protective bandages around the bottom half, to just below his knee. "It's just a pre-flight check. And a tiny, tiny treat. Just our little secret, eh Joe?" Joe turned to nudge her, always hoping for another treat, then he turned to watch over the stable door again when none arrived.

Maureen did my bandages, put my saddle on with the white saddle cloth underneath, then the bridle with two bits and unlocked the bolt to start my walk.

"Come on Marls," she coaxed, "let's get you warmed up. Can't do your gymnastics without a bit of a stretch."

Of course, I did not want to leave the barn without Joe and I danced impatiently tossing my head until Joe was ready. But with Sophie and Joe beside us we walked smartly off across the cinder path to a grass field where we walked around, slowly at first, then a few trots. The field was getting busy with horses and their humans, and the wind blew into my ears, making it difficult to concentrate.

"Malé's on his toes a bit this morning. Shall we trot on a bit more?"

So we did more trotting until Fiona arrived. Maureen panting from running by my side.

"Morning girls," she said. "How are they today?"

They chatted about the weather and how we had spent the night until Fiona said: "Right, we'll get mounted and do a bit of lateral work. We're well up the table so this one's a big thing to maintain our positions. Robin's horse doesn't do brilliantly at the dressage phase, and this is Pip's horse's first season at this level, so we should be off to a good start to put some pressure on everybody else. Malé can pull it back in the showjumping, and Joe in the cross country if we need a few more points, so I'm hopeful we'll end the season in the top five."

Sophie nodded. They both mounted and Maureen checked the girths were tight, and our work began. Round and round the grassy arena, showing our paces, faster, slower, bending, stopping, moving off again, all with our heads tucked in and with two bits in our mouths. Fiona nudged my sides and squeezed the reins and shifted her weight to tell me what I should do. At the end we always stop in the middle and Fiona drops her head towards the humans who watch, and then I know we are done. We walk out slowly and I can stretch my neck at last. Fiona jumped down in the outside arena and handed my reins to Maureen. Joe was steadily cantering in a circle on a loose rein, shifting from left lead to right as he turned to go in the other direction. Fiona watched, frowning a little.

"You won't get any points with reins like washing lines!" she said, as Sophie brought Joe to a smooth halt in front of us.

"Oh, yes, I know. I was just… we were warming up and.."

"That was a lovely transition, though, I have to say. Another three riders then you're on. Let me see some lateral work then have a break, so he's still fresh, OK?"

Sophie smiled and did as she was asked. Joe did too, and when Fiona finally nodded, Sophie stopped and dismounted to lead Joe about till it was their turn.

Back in the barn our stables were clean and there was fresh water and hay and our lunchtime feed to eat.

Joe dozed for a while, head drooped, one leg resting on the tip of his hoof.

"Try to rest Malé," he said.

"It's OK Joe, You sleep for a while. I'll watch."

Joe slept, woke, yawned and stretched and soon Sophie and Maureen returned. It was time for the fastest part of our work. The lighter saddles and simpler bridles with extra straps around our chests were put on. Sophie was dressed to ride, whilst Maureen had on her dark overalls. She placed her can on the locker outside the stable.

"Going's a bit slippy out there. You will be careful won't you?" Maureen said as she swung open the stable door.

"Still have to gallop or we'll be last back, and that wouldn't do at all!" she replied.

"I know but…just…go steady eh?"

"What's up Maur, would you miss me if I came to a sticky end out there?"

"You know I would." Maureen answered, "How would I look after both of them on my own?"

Sophie smiled and picked up her body protector from the locker as she passed.

"Do you think Fiona suspects?" Maureen asked.

"What?"

"That you've been riding him in that bitless thing and the saddle pad."

"She might, but she hasn't said anything, so I think we're still safe for now."

The cross country course was busy, especially at the start, with spectators sitting, standing and craning over the ropes for a better view of the horses as they set off to gallop down the slope to the first jump. The air smelt of leaves and of the water in the valley where we would jump in and out just after half way through, and of the damp earth after the rain.

Joe went first. At the bell he lunged forward and was into a gallop within 3 strides. Sophie, standing in the stirrups out of the saddle, crouched over Joe's neck, her face set in concentration as she guided Joe towards the first jump – a set of wooden barrels with bushes either side. Over and steadily down, just the right pace so as not to slip, and not to lose any time either. Two more jumps, into and out of the wood, then the sharp turn and a solid combination. Because of the rain, sand had been added to the take off and Joe's back hooves sank a little as he reached to clear the wooden jump. Bending towards the next, one hoof slipped, but Joe recovered and gathered himself for the next but there wasn't enough space and his front legs caught on the wood and he fell awkwardly on the other side, rolling over in the earth. Sophie fell clear and got up, but Joe stayed down.

I stopped. Eyes wide. Maureen glanced up at me, then around to find out what I was looking at, although there was nothing to see. The announcer's voice told her. The steward turned the waiting rider back and closed off the entrance with his rope, then walked around speaking to riders and grooms explaining that there had been a fall but we hoped to get things moving again soon.

Fiona hurried to Maureen's side. "Stay here and try and keep Malé calm. I'll go and find out what's going on. Maureen? Maureen?"

"Oh. Yes. Can't I go?" Her voice panic-striken.

"You'll be better staying here. Malé needs you. I'll be back in a few minutes. No more. I'm sure they'll be OK, try not to worry," and she hurried off to the tent where the stewards gathered.

A blue lighted vehicle went past, followed by a landrover, bumping over the grass.

Sophie was helped into the blue lighted vehicle by two green uniformed men, limping on her right leg, holding her left arm close.

The men in the landrover jumped out and ran to Joe. The steward at the fence knelt by Joe's head.

"What happened?"

"He slipped a bit landing over the first. Just wasn't enough space to pick up for the second."

"How did he land? Did he roll? Hit the jump?"

"Yes, I mean, he hit it with his hind legs on the way down. Rolled over once. Is he going to be OK?"

"Hopefully he's just winded but we can't take any chances. Wouldn't want to make any injury worse. Who's the owner?"

"Weston's. The stable girl rides this one. Mrs Weston competes on the black one. They go everywhere together."

"Right, get her down here. And a lorry, I want him at the hospital, I suspect a star fracture right hind cannon bone. Unlucky, but it does happen."

"Is he going to be OK?"

"We'll do what we can. This sort of thing can go either way. We need to keep him calm. I'm going to sedate him so we'll need help to lift him onto the lorry."

The steward turned and spoke into the radio.

Fiona flung open the door of the car. She covered the distance to where Joe lay in a few strides. "I'm Fiona Weston. The owner. Is he going to be OK?"

"Ah, Mrs Weston. I'm Jim Taylor, the course vet. I want to get your horse to the hospital for a proper assessment, some tests, x-rays certainly. I need your permission."

"Yes. I'm coming with you. He'll need his companion."

"They don't normally allow horses that aren't being treated to stay, Mrs Weston, but…"

"The job will be easier if you do, I assure you," Fiona answered briskly, and she stepped aside as the steward spread a large sheet out and began tucking it underneath Joe, who lifted his head briefly, and laid it back down again.

"It's OK Joe, we're going to sort this out," Fiona said, briefly stroking his nose before she strode back to the car.

"Did they take Sophie to hospital?" she asked the driver.

"The rider? No, I just got a message, she's in the first aid tent waiting for you. They wanted to take her to Sandbeck local but she's insisting she's fine. Typical of you riders. You think you're made of Teflon."

Fiona smiled in spite of the situation and made her way back to where Maureen waited, looking stiff and grim.

"Sophie's in the first aid tent. Sounds like she's fine. Joe's off to the hospital. I'll get Malé boxed up while you speak to Sophie then you can head up there together later on."

"What shall I tell her? Is Joe OK? Is Malé going to the hospital then?" she stammered, bewildered and on the verge of tears.

"Maureen, listen to me. I know how fond you are of Sophie, and I know this is going to be one of the hardest things I've ever asked you to do. I want you to tell her Joe is fine, tell her I'm with him and she can phone me as soon as we get to the equine hospital. You can bring her over later once we're clear about what needs to be done. She needs you to be strong right now, OK?"

Maureen nodded. Her eyes were bright with tears. Fiona squeezed her arm. They both tried to smile.

"Off you go. I'm on the mobile and I'll call as soon as I find out what's what. OK?"

I followed Fiona onto the lorry. It was strange without Joe, but when Joe did not finish his work as usual, I knew I must go to him, and although every instinct told me to run and find him, this time, trusting the humans was what had to be done.

Hospital

The lorry stopped at a new place with a wide tarmac car park. As we waited, I strained my ears to hear Joe. I heard a horse's hoofbeats and whinnied. The horse replied but it was not Joe. The lorry reversed closer to the buildings and the engine stopped. Fiona swung down from the cab and went over to the brightly lit office and spoke to the woman behind the computer screen. Then she came out and unbolted the right side of the big rear door, moved over to undo the left hand side. As the door dropped the woman came to meet Fiona and pointed out the stables in the small barn at the far end. Fiona nodded and undid the rope to lead me down the ramp. We walked over to where the woman had shown us. There were two empty stables. I was led into the one at the end. There was hay and water and thick rubber mats on the floor. Fiona bolted the stable door behind her and stayed at my head.

"Don't worry Malé," she said "it's all going to be OK. We must be strong for Joe, alright? You stay calm here and I'll go and find him. Good boy." She patted my neck and walked away.

Although I hated staying alone, and shoved and kicked at the door, it would not budge and I could only watch and wait until Fiona came back. She wasn't gone for very long.

"Good news Malé," she said, "Joe's nearly done. He'll be back next to you in a few minutes. Before you even know it." She stayed with me, talking quietly, until Joe appeared. He was not walking, but moving slowly along on a big wheeled trolley. One hind leg was covered in a large white bandage. I whinnied quietly, so as not to upset Joe. He lifted his head a little, but he could not say anything. He was moved into the next stable and put in a huge sling which held him up with a wide band around his belly tied to the frame over his head. Then the moving trolley was taken away. Joe's hooves just touched the floor, apart from the one with the bandage. That leg stayed off the floor. His head drooped and his eyes were half closed.

"Malé? Malé? Is that you?"

"Joe! Yes, it's me. The humans have brought me here to stay beside you until you are better."

"Good. That's good."

"Does it hurt?"

"Yes. My leg hurts. And my head. My back a little too."

"Try to rest. I'm here to watch."

"Yes. It smells strange here."

"It does."

"I wish we were out in the pasture again. Like when we were young."

"Yes, Joe. So do I. When we get home I hope they will let us go out again together."

Joe heaved a great sigh and his head dropped further. We did not speak any more until the moon had risen over the barn and silvery light made the white walls of the barn glitter like frost. I tried to eat some hay but it tasted of nothing. My food was left in the bucket. A stray leaf blew across the floor.

Despite the humans checking on Joe throughout the night, he did not speak much but dozed with his head hung low. As the moon shone and starlight twinkled outside Joe suddenly lifted his head and stared with wide eyes.

"Malé … Malé?"

"Yes Joe, I'm here. I'm in the next cage to you."

"Malé, the jumping. Running and jumping. Can't run any more. My leg hurts. Can't run. What will happen to me Malé? What will the humans do?"

"Shush, Joe, It's OK. I'm here. I'm right beside you."

Joe tied to move, but he couldn't go anywhere as the sling held him fast. He struggled, the metal frame crashing against the bars that separated us. A nurse came running. She ran back to the kitchen and returned with a needle, calling for her colleague. As Joe blundered about the stable she pressed it to his neck and stepped away. Joe's head dropped and his eyes, once wide in panic, now began to close.

"Can't run any more…." His breath came in short bursts. "Leg hurts… Malé!…"

"Joe. I'm here. The doors are locked, so we're staying here. It's safe. I am watching."

"But…. I can't run… what will they do… I can't run….can't run any more…"

"Joe! Listen to me. Remember Finn and Quest? Our friends in the field at home? They used to run and win races for the humans. And look at them now. They have their own field to rest in. No more work for them. We can stay with them when our work is finished. It's going to be fine, Joe. Both of us will stay with them. You and me. And we'll stroll by the stream again and eat all the best green plants and stand under the shade of the chestnut tree when the sun is strong. And in the winter we'll stay in the barn away from the wind. It's going to be fine Joe."

Joe's breathing was slower now, and steady. I had to eat. Joe needed me more than ever. I turned to the hay and concentrated on it for a while, chewing slowly, one eye on Joe. He had always looked out for me and I must not let him down when he needed me the most.

***

"They're in the end two stables. Joe's due a check in half an hour, so Mr Taylor will be over to speak to you." The woman from the office showed Sophie and Maureen where we were. I whinnied to them both.

"Malé! How are you old boy!" Sophie patted my neck. "And Joe! Oh, my goodness. He's in a sling. Have you ever seen anything like it before?" She turned to Maureen, open mouthed.

"Yes, but only once. That stallion that won the Oaks three times. They pulled out all the stops when he cracked a cannon bone slipping off the lorry at Kempton."

"Oh Joe!" Sophie put one arm around his neck and pressed her cheek to his.

"Looks like Fiona had words. They never let companions stay. More work for the staff."

"But if it helps Joe stay calm. It can't be very comfortable, that thing."

A girl came from the small kitchen at the end. She smiled at Sophie and Maureen.

"Hello, I'm Amanda. I'm on duty tonight so I'll be keeping an eye on.. Joe is it?"

"Josie's Bar of Gold," Maureen said. "Joe."

"Do you look after him then? At home I mean?"

"Yes. We're from Weston's."

Oh, Weston's with the racehorses? I didn't know you evented."

"I ride Joe and Mrs Weston rides Malé."

"Yes." She smiled at me. "We don't normally allow the able bodied to hang around, but Mrs Weston insisted."

"I'm sure she did," said Maureen.

"Are you OK?" she turned to Sophie. "Was it a fall?"

Sophie lifted her bandaged arm and nodded, wincing.

Amanda studied the chart hung outside Joe's stable. "He's still on the pain relief, but that's being re-assessed in the morning. Is he a good do-er?" she asked.

"Oh yes!" Maureen and Sophie answered together. "Our Joe will do anything for a sweet!"

"That's good," she nodded, relieved. "The sooner we get him eating again the better. As you'll know, microbial die off from the gut can trigger a toxic reaction. We can stop him getting dehydrated with a drip, and control the pain to some extent, but if they won't eat, it makes everything so much harder."

"Oh, I'm sure you won't have any trouble on that score." Maureen answered.

"Is there anything he particularly likes? Anything we can tempt him with?"

Sophie and Maureen exchanged glances. Amanda nodded. "It's OK, I won't tell anyone."

Maureen took a packet of mints from her pocket and handed it to Amanda. "He loves these. So does Malé."

Amanda tore open the mints and offered one to Joe. He sniffed it carefully, then licked it slowly from Amanda's hand. The sound of crunching made them all smile. "Oh, and one for you too!" I took a mint and remembered how hungry I was. Joe had not eaten since before our fast work had begun earlier that day. Since Joe began to show some interest in his surroundings, Amanda fetched a bucket of feed and offered him a small handful. I went back to my bucket. If I was going to be there for Joe I had to keep up my strength too. We ate together. Just a little.

"The sling allows him to move around a bit, we just need to keep that hind leg up off the floor until we can assess the damage. There's quite a lot of swelling, so once that's gone down, we'll get a better idea."

"How long will he be in it?" Maureen asked.

"Up to a week. Maybe a few days if the damage is minimal. Then we'll have to be sure he's fit to travel, you see."

"We'll look after him when he gets home."

"Of course." Amanda busied herself with gathering the drugs for Joe's next examination. I chewed the hay and watched.

***

"Fiona, what's going on? Where are you all?"

"I'm at the local hostelry having a drink and something to eat. I've had nothing since breakfast and it's gone 5 o'clock."

"I heard there'd been a fall. Are you all OK?"

"Of course. Joe slipped and fell at the barrels. Going was a bit soft and he lost his footing."

"Oh, so it was Sophie. Is she OK? And Joe?"

"Joe's at the local equine hospital, with Malé."

"What the heck is Malé doing there? He's OK right?"

"Yes, he's fine, but Joe will get better much quicker with Malé beside him."

"Fiona, you know they're not insured for eventing?"

"Of course they are."

"No they're not. My insurance only covers flat racing and national hunt at a recognized racecourse. It's going to cost a fortune having them both there. I'm surprised they allowed it to be honest."

"John, for goodness sake, you don't think I'd risk my best ever eventer by going out with no insurance do you?"

"But I thought we agreed, it was expensive so we weren't going to do it? Just the bare minimum."

"You agreed. I did it anyway."

"So… it's all covered? All of it?"

"Yes. I've spoken to the manager and he's going to put it all on the one claim. Malé's keep as well as Joe's medical care. Just add it on as stabling or something."

"Oh. Right. Good."

"Are you coming over? Can you bring Tig?"

"Tig? What for?"

"Just a hunch. Ask him if he wants to."

"OK. Oak View Equine Hospital?"

"Come to the pub in the village. The Red Lion. You can pick me up here."

"Right I'm on my way."

"Oh, and John, bring the painkillers from the drawer, will you?"

"Right you are." John replaced the phone on its cradle, rummaged through the drawer for the box of tablets, took the car keys off the hook in the hallway, picked up his wallet and flat cap from the kitchen table and went out, locking the farmhouse door behind him.

"Martin? Tig!"

"Yes boss?" Martin opened the tack room window and stuck his head out. "What's up? Is everyone OK?"

"I think so. Joe had a fall and he's in the local equine hospital."

"Joe?" Tig's voice came from behind Martin. "Is Sophie OK?"

Martin turned. "No-one's arranging a funeral, so I expect so."

Tig's yard boots thundered on the wooden steps as he took them two at a time down to the yard.

"Can I come, boss?"

"Oh, Tig, yes. Your presence has been requested, as it happens."

"Did Sophie ask for me?"

"No, it was Fiona actually, but you're welcome all the same. She who must be obeyed and all that. As long as we're back for Tuesday. You're up on the syndicate gelding this time."

"OK. Thanks."

"Martin? You're in charge till we get back. See you in the morning!"

As John pulled off the yard, turning on the headlights lit up the brown leaves on the beech hedge briefly before plunging them into shadows once again.

John turned to Tig as they swung onto the main road and picked up speed. "You know, sometimes, it's a blessing in disguise having a wife who takes not the blindest bit of notice of anything I say."

***

"We're over here!" Fiona waved as John appeared at the inner door of the pub, closely followed by Tig.

"Ah, yes. You got yourself a drink I see?"

"Of course. Would you like a shandy before we head off to the hospital? Tig? Anything for you?"

"Oh, just a coffee if they do that, Mrs Weston."

"I'll have coffee too."

"Maureen, do the honours would you? My card's behind the bar."

Maureen slid out from the cushioned bench and made her way to the bar. Tig took her place beside Sophie.

"Are you OK? What happened?"

"Oh, the ground was a bit soft between the combination and Joe slipped before we took off. Luckily I fell clear. He rolled right over."

"Were you knocked out?"

"Briefly. Maybe, I don't know. It's all a blur."

"Of course it is. These things happen so fast. Have you got the tablets, John?" Fiona asked.

He patted his top pockets and found the crumpled packet of painkillers.

"Here. Two every four hours."

Sophie picked up the tablets and gazed at them in her hands.

"Where does it hurt?" Tig asked gently.

"Everywhere. But mostly my arm." She dissolved into tears. Tig put his arm around her shoulders and pulled her as close as he dare, avoiding any pressure on her arm, still in a light sling across her waist. She sobbed quietly, with her head on his shoulder. Hot tears soaked his old checked shirt.

Fiona motioned to John, and he followed her obediently to the bar and Fiona brought back Tig's coffee, placing it carefully on the dark stained table.

"We'll leave you two to chat," she said and quietly left them.

Maureen glared. Tig glanced at her, then back to Sophie.

"It's OK. There now. It's going to be fine. Things will look different in the morning," he soothed, brushing Sophies long dark hair from her face.

"But Joe.... It's all my fault..." she sobbed.

"It's not your fault. Not at all. We all know the risks. Sometimes these things happen. And Joe's going to be OK. We're all going to be OK. There now. It's all OK."

As Sophie's tears finally subsided she wiped her face on the serviette that came with Tig's coffee.

He smiled at her. She returned his smile with a small one of her own.

Tig took a sip of his coffee. "Those tablets. They work you know."

Sophie thought for another moment, then opened the box and pressed two tablets from the strip. Tig pushed his coffee towards her.

"Thanks. It wasn't so bad earlier. It's absolutely caning now."

"It will be. It's the shock. It dulls the pain for a while."

Sophie nodded and grimaced as she swallowed hard.

"How long before they start to work?"

"Give it 15 minutes and you'll be dancing out of here! Looks like our Maureen is a little jealous."

"Jealous? I wouldn't think so. She never wanted to ride competitively. And with the state I'm in right now..."

"I didn't mean that." Tig's voice was quiet. "I mean. I mean, Maureen and me, we're both in love with you, but I think I've a far better chance than she has. If you see what I mean."

Sophie looked from Tig to Maureen and back again. Then down at the tablets in her hand.

"No pressure or anything. Just. Well, when I heard there'd been an accident my first thought was that I never got round to telling you how I feel."

Sophie's gaze rested on Tig's face. His green eyes, usually full of fun, were solemn.

"Look, I'm sorry. I shouldn't have said anything.. I just.."

"No. It's OK. It makes sense. I just….never wanted to admit it really. About Maureen. I love her to bits, she's the best friend I ever had. But I'm not… that way inclined."

Tig nodded, drank the rest of his coffee and offered Sophie his arm.

"Come on. Time to get you home."

***

John stretched and yawned. He took a large gulp of the strong black brew from the small white cup.

"So, you didn't ride the cross country then?"

"No. I had to be there for Joe and the girls. I couldn't have ridden not knowing what was going on."

"Shame, you were well up the table this year."

"We were, yes. Another top five placing would have put us in line for the top three with two to go."

"Maureen! You don't have a drink. What can we get you? To thank you for holding the fort today."

Maureen pressed her lips together and frowned. Glancing at the table where Tig and Sophie sat and back again, she said savagely: "I'll have a rum and coke, please, Mr Weston. Make it a double, if it's all the same to you."

Recovery

"So, you can see from the x-ray the shape of the fracture, radiating out from the impact. Looks like he knocked it pretty hard on the obstacle, but no other obvious injuries. He'll be a bit sore and bruised for a while of course, but I'd expect that to improve pretty quickly. As long as we can keep him calm and immobilized until there are definite signs of healing, the outlook is fair to good." The vet tapped the device to show Fiona and John the observations. "He's started eating a little, which is another good sign. He's very settled next to his companion, but they both got a bit upset when they were separated so the companion could get some fresh air."

"Yes. They've always been together. Mainly for Malé's benefit, but now it seems, Joe needs Malé more. Any indication of when they can come home? We have excellent facilities. Horse walker, nice big loose boxes. And both my girls are very experienced with managing things. They keep the yard running smoothly whatever gets thrown at them."

"Yes, I noticed. Sophie, isn't it? The nurse said she was giving Joe a neck massage."

"Did it help?" John asked.

"Seemed to," the vet replied, "though I'm not sure if was the fact that he knows Sophie or the massage really, but he's been very settled. Makes life easier. The horse walker might help too, once the injury has healed. You'll need to avoid anything strenuous until your vet has checked on it in about six weeks time.

Does your equine vet have a mobile x-ray, do you know?"

"Yes," John replied, "we had a mare with a suspected pedal bone fracture last year. Turned out to be just a deep seated abscess, so as soon as it was lanced she could put her hoof to the floor again."

"Yes, they like to worry you. And of course, abscesses can be nasty. Especially if they have to work through the tissue to find an exit point."

"About the bill…"

"Yes, Mr Weston, it's all in order. Your wife has made a down payment of £800 to cover the initial emergency work, and I'll get the interim invoice ready for you when you leave this evening, for the insurance company."

"OK. We'll get them primed."

"I've already called them. They're expecting the invoice. I've never needed to claim with this company before, but other riders have said they've been good about paying up," Fiona said.

"Always good to hear." The vet closed the device and got up.

"Right. If you'll excuse me, I must get on. I've an operation this evening. Recurrent colic on its way in."

"Yes, of course, thank you."

"Thank you." John added and watched as the young vet strode off towards the operating theatre. Several veterinary nurses passed them on their way in and out with trays of instruments and bandages and several large silver buckets, white cardboard boxes with drugs and syringes and tubes and a shiny silver trolley to line them all neatly up on.

"I've been thinking," Fiona said as they passed along the line of stables, mostly empty, across the white concrete floor scrubbed clean. "Maybe it's about time for Malé to start his stud career."

"Oh?" John answered, glancing at his wife.

"Yes. I mean, if it turns out that Joe isn't going to be able to event any more, I can't see it being worthwhile taking him all over the country with Malé next season. And you need Sophie at the yard, so taking her and Maureen away from the work so often doesn't seem very fair."

"Oh. Well…"

"And she is your employee after all."

"Yes. But…"

"So I'll make some enquiries, but I think we should aim for a stud fee of about a thousand pounds. Considering…"

"What?" John stopped and turned to face Fiona. "You mean, each time he does the deed we get a grand?"

"Possibly. Considering his sire. He'd appeal to people wanting national hunt horses and event riders as well, now he's got a few BE points and two good seasons under his belt. It's not easy finding a good thoroughbred sports horse sire, you know. We could even breed a couple ourselves. Start them off and sell them on. What do you think?"

"I think it's a smashing idea. Might even get a return on our investment."

"I thought you'd like that idea," Fiona smiled, "and all that fence building was worth it after all. It's much better when people can see him actually working."

"He does look the part, I must say."

They reached the stables where Joe was now out of the sling and standing quietly eating hay. He could only move slowly on his injured leg, which was covered in a think padded bandage from above his hoof to his hock. Joe whickered gently at the humans he had known all his life.

"Hello, old boy. How are you today? We're going to get you home soon. Back to your own stable until you're better. How does that sound eh?" Fiona stroked Joe's nose. She rummaged in her pocket for some mints. "Here we are. Have a chew on that."

"What about Malé? I can't believe you gave Joe a sweet without him."

"Of course. And how are you my lovely? You've done a grand job taking care of Joe. But we need to get you both home very soon." She rubbed my cheeks.

Amanda joined them. "Ah, Mrs Weston. Mr Weston. I'm glad I've seen you. I'm just about to go, just finished my night shift and Mr Taylor said Joe's ready for the journey home, so I may not see them again."

"I hope not," John said. "I mean, you've done a marvellous job, but it's time they came home."

"It is. Mr Taylor will explain, but basically, he needs to rest as much as possible, but start some gentle walking, just five minutes a day, take it at his pace, then increase gradually. He can come off the sedatives after a week, as long as he stays calm. I've written it all up for you."

"Thank you," said Fiona. "Thank you for all you've done. He's a lovely horse. We'd all miss him so much if… well… he's such a character."

"Oh he is. I've enjoyed looking after him. And I've learnt a lot from your stable girl. She came and gave him a massage, to help him relax. I'm going to ask if I can go on a course, so I can help a few more horses. They can get so tense with all the treatment they have to have sometimes. It can't be easy for them."

"No, it can't be easy. Sophie is marvellous, isn't she? We're so glad to have her. She'll be looking after Joe when he gets home too."

"That's good to hear. Well, I'd better go and get some sleep."

"Yes. Do. And thank you again."

Amanda smiled as she left the barn and another of the nurses came to explain about Joe's journey home and what medication he needed.

And when the best horse-box was reversed up to the big doors, Joe and me both knew it was time to go home.

New life

It was so good to get home. Even our cages didn't seem so bad when we looked out over the half doors at the same view, same horses, and life began to settle into a new routine. The smell of the hospital hung around in our fur for days, and we could not get out to roll in the damp earth.

Fiona stopped by our stables one day and looked thoughtfully across at Joe's side as she swept the damp shavings into a corner for Sophie and Maureen to clear later.

"John!" she called as she stood the broom up outside my cage and bolted the door. "What do you think if we removed the barrier between Joe and Malé's stables?" John put his mobile phone back in his inside pocket.

"What? Completely?"

"Yes. Well if they're going to have to be in there for another couple of weeks I think it might help if they can actually see each other properly."

"Oh. OK. Worth a try."

"And I'll need a pen for them in the field with the oldies, so they can't gallop up and down like lunatics."

"Good idea. Get Joe moving a bit. I'm surprised they've coped so well after being at peak fitness to suddenly immobile. And some doctor green grass never hurts."

"Right. I'll get Fred onto it. And order some posts from Duggins. It'll be a good place for any visiting mares later on."

They walked back towards the farmhouse together.

***

"So, you don't miss the competition life then?" Tig asked as he and Sophie sat at the window in the village pub.

"Not really, no. I kind of fell into it because of Malé being so close to Joe. It wasn't something I was desperate to do."

"Oh. So what will you do now? Won't going back to yard work seem boring?"

"Not at all. Looking after Joe has been quite hard really, getting the tablets down him and making sure he's not going to undo everything by running off. And I've noticed a change in him. Since the accident. He doesn't seem his usual happy-go-lucky self."

"Hmmm... Yes. I've noticed he doesn't want to leave Malé now, and it used to Malé who was the clingy one."

"Exactly. They've been through a lot together."

Sophie stared into her lemonade for a moment and then her gaze wandered around the room, the familiar bar crammed with pictures of hunting scenes, old horse brasses and coloured glass ornaments. She turned her attention back to Tig, who smiled at her.

"What?" she asked.

"Don't try and tell me there isn't a plan or three in that brain of yours. I can see it all over your face."

"Well...."

"You can tell me. I'm never one to trample on someone's dreams."

"Well. I thought of that place down South. The one where they rehab those horses."

"Brickyard Farm? I've heard of it. One of the jockeys went there to visit a horse with his mum. Her old hunter with a pulled tendon. Came back 6 months later as good as a four year old again."

"Yes. That's the place. It's what they do. Do you think…" Sophie stopped and gazed at Tig, who took a sip of his orange juice and smiled back at her.

"Well, I've been offered a lift down there, with the teacher from that course I went on. She does articles and wants to see a case study of theirs. Would you come with me?"

"What about Maureen?"

"It's not her kind of thing. She'd just be bored and…"

"And?"

"Well, there might be a job going there. At Brickyard Farm. I'd love to work there. Then, if the chance came up, to open my own place and do the same kinds of things. For racehorses and eventers who get injured and that kind of thing."

"But can't you do that kind of thing here?"

"No. It's different. They don't use shoes or operations. It's all barefoot and working out how to help the horses heal by themselves."

"Tell me when and I'll ask the boss."

"Great. Thanks, Tig. You're a star." Sophie beamed, drank the last of her lemonade and stood up, picking up her faded blue hoody. "Come on, we're up early tomorrow. Better get some zeds in. Aren't you riding Greensleeves?"

"I am. In the two o'clock. Then Regimental Master after that."

"Ooh, aren't we going up in the world!" Sophie teased.

"I sincerely hope so!" he replied, putting his arm around her shoulders as they left for the walk home.

***

"So what do you think? Are you up for it, Maur?"

"Up for what?"

"You know what. The show at Brin Hill."

"Who's going?"

"Me, Martin, Mike…"

"Is he going?"

"He?" Sophie lifted her head from her magazine and frowned at Maureen. "If you mean Tig, then possibly, yes. Depends on whether they're back from Southwell in time the day before."

"I'll give it a miss then, if it's OK with you."

"Well, no, actually, it's not. We always go to these things together. Why won't you come?"

"I'm not up for being the third wheel, Soph."

"You wouldn't be. Tig and Martin will more likely just find the best beer tent and stay there all afternoon. I want you to come with me."

"Well, you can't always have everything you want. Life's a bitch, remember?"

"Maureen!" Sophie looked hurt and stared at her best friend open mouthed.

"You go off and have a good time with your new bessie mate, don't worry about me."

The silence hung as Maureen huddled over her smartphone.

"Alright, have it your way. But if you change your mind, you know where I am." She stood down from the stool she was sitting on and wound her way through the tables across the tack room to the stairs. She turned to look at Maureen, her hand on the smooth white rail, but Maureen pretended to be busy with something unmissable on her phone.

Sophie sighed and made her way down the stairs.

"You'd better sort your head our Maureen, before you lose her entirely." Martin looked up from his newspaper.

"And who asked you?" Maureen spat back, haughtily.

"Tig's a nice lad. She could do a lot worse."

"He's a crap jockey."

"If you mean he'd rather bring a horse in second than beat them past the finishing post, then yes, some might say he's a crap jockey. But that's not what it's about for John and Fiona. John's turned down owners who just want to win. It's the new thing. Animal rights and all that."

"Great. So we'll all be out of job at some point then."

"Even racing has to move with the times. And you know what I'm talking about Maureen, so don't change the subject."

"I don't care what you're talking about Martin, if Sophie wants to waste her life with a loser, that's her problem."

"Rather than waste it with you, you mean?"

Maureen got up from her chair with such force that it fell backwards, knocking over the round table next to it. Magazines scattered, loose pages spreading out across the dusty floor.

"Bastard!" she shouted, stumbling out of the room pushing over anything in her way. She thundered down the stairs, ran across the yard to the car park, wrenched open her car door and was gone in a moment.

John appeared out of the farmhouse and made his way up the stairs.

"What was all that about?" he asked Martin.

"Tempers frayed a little, boss," Martin said. "Our Maureen doesn't like feeling like the third wheel."

"And who could blame her." John replied. "Are they going to be OK? We need them both. Sophie and Maureen. They've always worked so well together. Shame if it all went tits up for the sake of a teenage love affair."

"Oh, I think you'll find Tig's in it for the long haul. He's no fool. Knows a good thing when he sees it. It'll be fine, boss. Just give them all time to get their heads around it."

"Yes, Tig too. He's a lot of potential as a jockey. Specially for the more modern owners. And we'll be getting a few more of those by the looks of things. I don't want any tension when they all want to call in for a visit to pat their newest investment."

"There won't be. I'll see to it."

"Thanks, Martin. I'll leave it with you, then. Now, next week's schedule."

Arrested

"Sophie? Soph? Are you coming? Martin's about to leave." Tig knocked on Sophie's door and pressed his ear to the wood.

"Come in, I'm ready. Just about."

Tig smiled as he went in to find Sophie hunched over on the old vinyl tub chair in the corner or her tiny room. She lifted her head and he saw she had been crying.

"Soph! What's up? What's happened?" He sat down on the end of the bed opposite her. She stared at her smartphone, sniffed and handed the device over.

Tig read. "Dear Miss Jones, thank you for your application for the position of groom at Brickyard Farm. After careful consideration we regret to inform you....Oh. Right."

Sophie rung the tissue in her hands and sniffed some more.

"I'm really sorry Soph. I know how much you wanted that job."

"No, it's OK. Really. I love it here. There's plenty to do. And if I'd got it, well, you'd be that much further away, I'd hardly get to see you."

"Sophie, you know I'd.."

"Are you two coming? We'll miss the main event if you don't get a move on!" Martin's voice called up the stairs.

"Just a mo, Martin," Tig called back.

"Come on. Let's go and have some fun. Forget about this place. Jobs. All of that. It's their loss."

"I know. But…"

"I know." He glanced down at the phone again and stared at the rejection email. "You know they had over a hundred and fifty applications?"

"Wait. What?" Tig passed her phone and Sophie read the rest of the email. "A hundred and fifty! Blimey."

"And I bet you were number two on the list too."

At last, Sophie smiled. "Time for some fun. Yes. Let's do it."

***

The journey was over an hour through the lanes lined with hedges and trees, their leaves turning red and yellow and orange, bright with berries for birds and small mammals to gorge on in preparation for the cold months ahead. The car bumped slowly along the roughly mown field car park until Martin stopped next to an old landrover, applied the handbrake and killed the engine.

"Here we are. Our playground for the next five hours, people."

"Oh, your window's open Martin," Sophie pointed.

"I know. I tell it to stay up but whatever I say it always falls down that inch."

"OK. Trip to the garage then?"

"At some point yes. Next payday perhaps. Jockeys hardly ever get rich, you know. Right. Everyone got their stuff? I'm going to be holed up in the best beer tent for a while so if you want anything from the car grab it now."

The four of them made their way up the hill to the entrance. There was a short queue while the spectators each bought their tickets and programmes, commented on how nice the weather was for the time of year, then moved on to join the crowds across the venue, hitching their bags over their shoulders and peering at the map on the centre pages as they went.

"Right. What's it to be first? Looks like there are three arenas. All the stalls are round the edges, by the looks of it."

"Let's just walk round and look first. Then decide."

"Right."

The crowds grew as they passed the main arena which was full of vintage tractors trundling slowly around, steam hissing as it rose from a polished brass chimney and fumes bellowing from the exhaust of another. Stalls selling saddles and jackets, boots and hats and even flooring tiles for stables, along with plenty of food vans and four large marquees, two at each end bustling with hungry spectators.

"Baked potatoes. Now that'll line our stomachs," Martin suggested, nodding towards the stall.

"Ooh yes, I'll have mine with beans and cheese." They queued and bought their food, then sat at the wooden trestle table covered in plastic table cloths, eating with plastic knives and forks, opening cans with a hiss.

"Cheers!" said Martin. "To Weston's and all who sail in her!"

"Cheers!"

When the last mouthfuls of potato were gone, the cans emptied, the napkins crumpled, Martin stood up, clambered out from the bench and announced: "Right I'm off to find out where the best beer is being served. And once I've found it, I'm not leaving till my boots are full!"

"And I shall join you Sir!" Mike added. "And if the rum is not as fine as a filly's ass, why there will be a song and dance, as I stand before ye in me best breeches!"

Tig shook his head and winked at Sophie. They rejoined the crowd and made their way slowly past a five piece brass band, in matching red waistcoats and braces. Martin grinned and began singing along. "Oh oh oh Gino…"

Mike joined in, playing an air trombone, a look of concentration on his unshaven face, blowing his cheeks out with each note. Martin followed suit playing an imaginary drum, and Tig turned and walked backwards facing Sophie with his thumb in his mouth wiggling his fingers across his imaginary saxophone. They fell in step, in time to the music, Martins surprisingly fine voice their only contribution to the music. A few spectators smiled and clapped as they passed. Sophie laughed at them all. One of the band members winked and the drummer threw his sticks in the air catching them between one beat and the next. Martin spotted a sign: "Cool beer. Apply within," he read out loud. "Right you are, me hearties.

At your service!" stopping short so that Mike blundered into him.

"We'll see you at the exit at six," Martin said and disappeared into the cool dark interior of the marquee. Mike hurried after him with a wave at Sophie and Tig, air trombone quickly discarded.

"Did you like my saxophone playing?" Tig asked.

"Oh, it was OK," Sophie told him. "But you missed a B flat in the chorus."

"Damn. You noticed." Tig tried to look devastated.

"You play the fool better."

"You're probably right."

They walked on, Tig with his arm around Sophie's waist.

There was so much to see, the time went quickly. They ended up at the main arena in time for the open jump-off. The clouds had built up a little, blocking the sun and making the air cool as they passed. Sophie got out her hoody, slipped her slim arms into it and zipped it up.

"Let's go a bit further down where it's less crowded," she suggested.

It was quieter and although the view was not as good, they could just see all the jumps if they stood up.

An older couple sitting quietly outside their car with flasks of coffee, which smelt slightly of whisky, offered them a camping chair each and they accepted gratefully. It was a big event and they'd walked quite a way seeing all the sights and were grateful for a rest.

They chatted politely about the weather and the show for a while and discovered that the couple had once both show-jumped and still had their last elderly horse living quietly with them until the end.

A shadow passed and stopped behind them. Sophie turned to find a steward on horseback alongside them.

"That's the one we saw at Field Farm," Sophie whispered to Tig.

The grey horse twisted his head and twitched, his mouth strapped tightly closed.

"I'm very sorry, but you can't park here. We don't allow cars on this part of the site. Health and Safety. You'll have to move."

"Oh dear," the elderly man got up and faced the steward who had dismounted from his horse, his yellow badge pinned to his lapel.

"We were told we would be allowed, as we're both disabled now, you know." The man pointed to his blue badge in the windscreen.

"I'm very sorry, but it's the rules. I don't know who told you it was OK, but it's definitely not. You'll need to pack up and make your way to the small car park right away."

Tig intervened. "Oh, they're not doing any harm, and there's only a few left in the jump off. I'm sure nobody would mind if..."

"Well I mind!" the steward interjected. "It's in the information you were sent. Didn't you read it?"

Sophie got up and began to fold the chairs they had been sitting on. The lady looked a little flustered, and quite upset. "We'll help you, don't worry," Sophie reassured her. "It won't take a minute."

"Thank you dear," the lady replied. "That's very kind."

Tig faced the steward, his mouth in a thin line. He stepped forward and spoke quietly.

"I think it's a bit harsh. Could you not just turn a blind eye for once? Really, it's nearly over. They oldies were enjoying the show not bothering a soul."

The steward drew in a breath. "I think you should mind your own business young man. I'm here to help keep order. I was told there's no parking here so off you go."

"Now, come on. Bending the rules won't hurt just this once, surely?"

The steward's mouth twisted in a sneer. "I'll thank you to help your friends do as they've been told and get off the site. And not tell me how to do my job!"

Tig stepped towards the steward and opened his mouth to speak. The grey horse raised his head and took a step back. The steward raised his whip and smacked the horse in the face.

"No!" Sophie flew from behind the car and flung herself between the steward and the whip, raised to beat the horse again. The solid end caught Sophie in the face as the steward swung it at them both and as the whip made contact with the side of her face she cried out and bent over, both hands holding her eye. Tig grabbed the steward by his jacket and dragged him away from Sophie and the terrified horse, who realized he was no longer held and bolted away from

241

them, reins and stirrups flying. The steward raised his whip and swung it towards Tig aiming at head height. One punch later and the steward fell backwards in the long grass like a bale of hay with the strings cut.

"Oh dear.... Oh dear." The lady dithered. Her husband put his arm around her shoulders. "It's alright dear. Looks like he's out cold. It's OK. Let's just sit for a minute."

"Oh my dear, are you OK?" she said to Sophie as she straightened herself up and looked at her hands, her breaths shallow and fast, her mouth open.

"Let me look!" Tig demanded. "The bastard. I'll..."

"No, Tig. Leave it. Stay here. Please."

A couple of spectators passed by and a few more gathered. A vehicle arrived and another steward jumped out.

"What the hell's going on here. Who did this?"

"I did." Tig said quietly. "He was coming at me with that whip."

"It was self-defence. For sure. Horrible man. Beating a horse like that!" the lady spoke up.

"We can't let things like this happen. If the sponsors find out bang goes our contract for next year."

"Why do you let someone like that steward? There's no excuse to treat a horse like that," Sophie added.

"Oh my goodness, what happened to your eye? It's actually bleeding. I'll get someone down here." The steward spoke into his radio. "Better send the ambulance. We've two casualties. One's out cold.... Yes, now!"

"I'm alright," Sophie protested. It's just a cut. Really."

"Best get it checked out, Soph, you never know. You can't be too careful with eyes." Tig advised, his voice concerned.

"Yes dear. Let them have a little look. I'm sure it will be fine, but there's no harm in letting them check," the lady added.

"You'll have a right black eye in the morning, by the looks of it," the steward said, replacing his radio in the top pocket of his yellow hi-vis jacket.

Tig shook his right hand, red marks appearing on his knuckles. The steward glanced at Tig. Tig turned away. The old man took a flat brown flask from the pocket of his tweed jacket. "Here son," he said. "There'll be questions asked. Have a swig of this to steady your nerves. I find it very helpful in these situations."

Tig took the flask and a swig, grimaced and coughed and handed it back.

"Oh, it's good stuff. None of your cheap supermarket slops" the man nodded knowingly.

The St John's ambulance rumbled slowly towards them and stopped. The driver and crew member got out. They and the steward busied themselves lifting their colleague carefully from the grass onto the stretcher.

"After three. One – two – three."

The steward groaned. "You've had a fall, Ron, we're getting you up to first aid to get checked out," the second steward said, loudly, close to Ron's ear.

"Bloody horse. I'll thrash him when I get him home. Never was any good." He tried to get up from the stretcher. "Calm down Ron," the crew members soothed. "You just relax and we'll get you sorted in no time."

He half sat up, caught a glimpse of Tig and Sophie, and began to shout "And you, you little shit, I'll teach you to interfere in my business…just you wait… I'll have the police onto you."

The ambulance doors shut. The driver nodded at Sophie. "Want me to have a look at that while we're here?"

"Not really," Sophie replied.

"Yes!" said Tig and their new friends.

The crew member sat Sophie on a camping chair and knelt beside her. He shone a light in both eyes. "Can you see alright? Yes? OK. Point to where it hurts," he asked, and when Sophie did he gently pressed her cheekbone. Sophie flinched. "Ouch!" she protested.

"Caught you right underneath the eye. You'll need it checked out by a doctor in the morning but I can't see any damage to your eye. And the cheekbone's very unlikely to be broken. Take it easy for a bit, OK?"

"Yes. I will." Sophie said.

"You'll make sure she's OK, right?"

"Course," said Tig, nodding.

"Any problems, straight to Accident and Emergency."

The driver climbed into the ambulance and waved as they pulled away.

Sophie turned to Tig.

"What now?"

"I reckon we should find the others and head off home. It's nearly six anyway."

"Right."

They thanked their new friends and walked quietly away.

At the exit two police officers were waiting.

Friends

"So. Mr….?"

"MacCauley. Mark MacCauley. Tig."

The police officer typed carefully, peering towards the screen.

"Tell me what happened."

"Well, the steward, Ron I think he's called, came over to tell the old couple to move their car. I asked him to leave them alone. They weren't doing any harm. He got annoyed and smacked the horse, so Sophie…"

"Miss Jones, right?"

"Yes. Sophie Jones. She got in between them and caught the whip right in the face. He nearly had her eye out."

Tig paused. The officer typed.

"And what happened next?"

"I grabbed him, to make sure he didn't hit anyone else and he went for me."

"With the same whip?"

"Yes. A hunting whip. The wedge end's made out of wood. For opening gates. You don't hit anyone with it."

"Yes. Go on."

"Well, he went for me, so I punched him. He went over. Out like a light. I didn't mean to hit him that hard. It all happened so quick."

The officer finished typing and turned the screen round.

"Read through everything and if you're happy with it, click the accept button at the end."

The clock ticked as Tig read. Then he nodded. "Yep. Done."

"You'll now be asked to wait until the duty sergeant has had a look through everything. Then, if there's no grounds for a charge, you can both go home."

"A charge? It was self-defence!"

"I understand. But it's not my call. I'll take you through to the custody suite until it's processed."

"What?" Tig was suddenly scared. "He attacked me. And Sophie. And the horse, dammit!"

"I know Mr MacCauley, so you say. It will all be sorted out soon enough. Now, if you'll follow me."

"Can I see Sophie?"

The officer raised his eyebrows. "I shouldn't really, but, you seem like a good kid. Come on, we'll go through reception. Your girlfriend should be finished in the interview room by now."

The heavy door opened. The officer waved Tig through and held the door open.

"Oh Tig. Are you OK?"

"Never mind me, how's your eye?"

"Really sore." She glanced at the officer behind the counter. "It really hurts" she said loudly. "And I'm a bit worried about it. My eye. Can we go now?"

"No, I've got to stay. Till the sergeant's had a read through. Then it'll be fine and we can go home."

"Mr MacCauley?" another officer came through the thick security door, glancing at his clipboard. "This way please."

248

***

Maureen typed into her ipad and smiled. She picked up her lukewarm coffee and cupped it in her hands. Her phone rang. She rolled over on her bed and picked it up from the floor. "Mike. What do you want?....He did what? What the hell. Where are you? Is Soph with you? Her eye? Shit. I'm on duty. Fiona's out." She stood up and strained to see out of the tiny window. "Wait, there's a light on in the farmhouse. John might be in. I'm on my way. Text me the postcode." She forced her feet into her trainers, squashing the heels, pulled on her yard jacket and hurried down the stairs and across the yard to the farmhouse.

"John? Are you in?"

"Yes. Doors open. What's up?"

"I'm not sure. Mike and the crew are stuck somewhere over at Markham apparently. I keep telling Martin to get that car fixed. Must have broken down."

"Are they all alright?"

"Oh yes. They seemed to be. Apart from the car. Can you hold the fort while I go and get them?"

"Yes. Sure. Anything I need to do?"

"No, everyone's been fed and watered. I'll do my night-time check when we're back. OK?"

"OK. See you later."

John sank back onto the settee and grabbed the remote control, and his beer, from the floor.

***

"Ah, Sarge. Before you knock off, there's this alleged assault. What do you want me to do?"

The sergeant took the clipboard from his constable and scanned through it, flicking through the first few pages.

"Hmmp. Ron Jameson. From Broughton. I know him. Right nasty piece of work by all accounts. My lass used to ride with his daughter."

"Oh."

"Yes, not above knocking his missis about after a day out with the Old Berkshire."

"Oh. I see."

"Looks like he lost it and someone gave him a taste of his own medicine. Who's the young lad?"

"Don't know the name Sarge."

"So he's not your regular thug then?"

"Doesn't look the sort. Nothing came up on the search. No previous."

"And no permanent damage done to Jameson?"

"Not at all, he's had plenty to say for himself. So nothing wrong with him really."

"Oh yes, he's full of it is our Ron. Let the lad go with a warning."

"No charges?"

"None at all, Jameson had what was coming to him in my view. Shame the lad didn't give him a proper hiding. It would have been his just desserts."

"He was just protecting the girl I think. Jameson was out of control."

"Precisely. Now if you'll excuse me, I've a Sunday roast and a glass of red waiting for me." He signed the papers and handed the clipboard back.

"Sir," said the constable, nodding as the sergeant made his way towards the back door of the station to his car.

"Miss Jones?" Sophie stood up from the vinyl chair in the waiting room, clutching her rucksack. "I'm going to fetch your friend now. The sergeant said no charges."

"Oh, thank you!"

"If you'll just wait here I'll go and spread the good news." He smiled and disappeared behind the security door. Sophie breathed a sigh of relief and sat back down again. Briefly closing her eyes. The outside door opened and Maureen peered in. Sophie gasped.

"Maureen! What are you doing here? How did you know?"

"Mike called me." They stood awkwardly for a moment.

"Oh Maur, I'm so glad you're here." Maureen held out her arms and Sophie ran and hugged her friend tightly.

"I'm so sorry. For what I said. For being such an arse. Will you forgive me?"

"There's nothing to forgive. It's fine. Really."

"I just… I just couldn't bear the thought of losing you forever."

"Me neither. You're the best friend I ever had, Maur. You're not getting rid of me that easily. Whatever happens I'll be here for you."

"Same." Maureen smiled at her friend, relieved. "So, who are you waiting for?"

"Tig's been in custody.."

"What?"

"I know. It's so unfair. That Ron bloke was coming at him with a hunting whip."

"Was that the one he caught your eye with, by any chance?"

"Yes. That one. I don't think Tig meant to stick one on him with quite such force, but the guy went over like a skittle."

Maureen stifled a giggle.

"It's not funny, Maur." Sophie tried to sound severe, but broke into a smile.

"I know, but he's not a nice man, by all accounts. That Ron bloke. I reckon there's a few round here would form an orderly queue to give him a bit of a hiding."

"Where are Martin and Mike?"

"Oh, they're still in the car park. Sobered up a bit. Wandered off to the garage to buy coffee, but they're back now."

"Coffee. I could murder one."

"We'll stop on the way…"

The heavy door creaked open and Tig appeared. His face fell as he saw Maureen.

"Tig. Are you OK?" Sophie held out her hand.

"Course." He hitched his rucksack over his shoulder as he took Sophie's hand. "What's the plan then? Did you drive here, Maureen? Is anyone with you?"

"I came on my own. Fiona's out on the town. John thinks Martin's car broke down. And… well... he can carry on thinking that as far as I'm concerned."

"Oh, thanks, Maur!" Sophie hugged her friend again. "Let's just get out of here."

"Right," Tig nodded. "I'll drive Martin's car then. Or we'd be in trouble if we got stopped. Both of them have had a skinful. Soph, why don't you travel back with Maureen? We'll see you back at the yard." He leaned to kiss Sophie's cheek and walked quickly towards the door.

"Thanks, Tig," Maureen said quietly.

"Thank you!"

"Come on, let's find that garage. We've had nothing to eat since a baked potato at lunchtime."

"And I bet you didn't fill up with beer, right?"

"We didn't, no. I wonder if they do sandwiches."

They walked back to the car, Sophie's arm through Maureen's, discussing their day.

***

"Oh, bloody hell, who's that at this time of the evening." John pressed the remote control button to silence the TV, flung it on the settee and leaned over to pick up the house phone. "Hello? Lower Barn Farm, John Weston speaking. Mr… sorry, who did you say you were? OK. Yes, how can I help you? Is there a problem?" John turned back towards the TV. "Oh, yes, the show. Some of my staff have spent the day there…. What do you mean? Which young man?

253

Look, I don't know why you've called me on a Sunday evening but… Oh. OK. I see…. Yes, they're all short, they're jockeys, Mr…."

"Oh Jooo-ohnnn, where are you my darling? My beloved? Have you missed me?" There was a crash as Fiona tripped over a chair in the kitchen. "Oooh! You naughty chair" she scolded, giggling. "John, darling, are you there? It's meeeee, your Foofy-woofy…"

"You're drunk!" he removed his hand from over the phone. "Yes, Mr…er…. Yes, I understand. I'll have a word in the morning. I have to go. Thank you. Yes. OK. I'll see to it. Bye."

"Johnny-wonny! Fiona lurched towards John. He caught her and dropped the phone over the back of the settee.

"Come along, let's get you to bed. Looks like you've had a marvellous time out with the girls."

"Oh I have. A marvelloush time. Do you know Marcia has a new girlfriend? I've missed you sooooo much. Gizza kiss…"

"Come on. Let's get you to bed and I'll get you a glass of water before you fall asleep."

"No-one had better phone again. I want you all to myshelf…my lovely Johhny-wonny-pooey-wooey.."

"Yes, OK. Let's just get you to bed. Time for that later."

Fiona leaned on John as he led her to the bedroom.

"My, these shtairs are sheep. Sht…shteers…." Fiona gave up trying to speak in favour of laughter, and by the time John had helped her take off her shoes and got her into bed, then got back from the bathroom with her glass of water, she was fast asleep, snoring quietly with her blue silk scarf over her face.

John sighed, shook his head, left the water on the small table next to his wife and went back to the TV.

The credits rolled. "Bloody hell. I'll never know whodunnit now!"

Rescued

Fiona rolled over and winced as the light hit her eyes. She groaned as the pain in her head erupted. Dragging herself to a sitting position, shoving the pillow behind her, she saw the glass of water John had left the night before. After briefly debating with her stomach she drank the whole glass and groaned again.

"John! John, are you there?" No answer, so Fiona swung her legs over the side of the bed, fishing for her slippers but giving up and making the short trip to the bathroom seem like a marathon. She stood under the hot shower and began to feel more alive. Dressing in her jeans and t-shirt, then her comfiest fleece she went to the kitchen.

"Thank god. Coffee." She poured herself a cup and sat at the kitchen table eyes half closed. The phone rang.

"Lower Barn Farm, Fiona speaking…. One of the jockeys? Oh, you'll need to speak to my husband…. Oh. One of our jockeys? It sounds like him, yes, but…. Right. I shall have a word Mister… Jameson. I'll call you back when I've spoken to my husband. Thank you. Bye."

The phone rang again.

"Lower Barn Farm, Fiona speaking."

"Ah, Mrs Weston. It's Bob Marks here, Maria's dad."

"Oh, er… Maria with Major, the coloured horse? Yes. How can I help?"

"Well, Mrs Weston, it's like this you see. Your young lass and her fella were involved in a bit of a...well, altercation yesterday at the show, and I wanted to tell you about what happened, like, so as you didn't get the wrong end of the stick."

"Yes, I heard about the.. altercation. I was just on my way to speak to the staff about it when you rang."

"Yes, well. What really happened Mrs Weston was, that your young rider, dark-haired girl, pretty lass, rides your chestnut gelding?"

"Sophie, yes?"

"Sophie. Well, she copped it from that Ron Jameson chap, right in the face with his hunting whip. He was going to smack the horse again and she ran right in there and he hit her with it instead. He's a nasty piece of work him, all nice and smarmy to folks' faces and behind closed doors he's nothin' but a bully. Friends of mine let him buy that grey horse, regretted it from day one, but it was too late, with his money in the bank."

"I'm not sure I follow. Do you mean Jameson was beating the horse? And Sophie got in the way?"

"More'n got in the way, she ran right in there and got between 'em. Wasn't having him abuse that animal in front of her. And then, you see, well..."

"Go on, Mr Marks."

"Her young man tried to restrain him, and Jameson went over like a skittle. Bullies never argue with anyone their own size, see."

"Yes, I see. And the horse, was he OK? I've seen him up at Field Farm when we've been training there."

258

"He's as well as a horse that's used to taking a beating can be, Mrs Weston. I'd have him myself, but I've had run-ins with that one before and he wouldn't let me on his yard no more, let alone sell me his horse."

"Yes." Fiona plumped down on the sofa and stared out of the window. "Yes, sorry Mr Marks. I think I'll go over there and see what I can do. What do you think?"

"I think if anyone can get that horse off his hands, it might well be you. Mrs Weston. He never has a bad word to say about yourself, not that I've heard anyways. And your staff, they'll not be in trouble over this, I take it? It weren't nothing nasty on their part. But seeing him treat that horse like that…well, there's many would have turned a blind eye, but not your Sophie and her young man. They're good people, Mrs Weston. I hope you'll bear it in mind when you have a word."

"I will, Mr Marks, of course. Thank you so much for letting me know. Give my regards to Maria, and Major."

"Oh I will, and thank you. I had to call. Couldn't leave it knowing what had happened and not saying, like."

"Yes. Thanks again. Bye."

Fiona replaced the phone in its white plastic cradle and looked out of the window, frowning. She got up and rummaged in the kitchen drawer for some paracetamols, swallowing two at once with a gulp of black coffee and headed out to the yard.

John had just finished the daily brief with the staff.

"Ah, Fiona. I wasn't expecting you to surface until lunchtime. How's your head?"

Fiona smiled weakly. "It's throbbing like a combine harvester at the moment, but the coffee should sort it out. Listen, can you spare Sophie for an hour? I just need to pop in and see someone about a horse."

"Oh, another mare? Malé's got a full schedule this month, you know."

"No, not a mare, as such. So, is it OK? I promise we'll be back for lunch."

"You'd better ask Maureen. She'll be left with the mucking out."

"OK. I will."

Sophie was on her way back from the muck heap, humming quietly to herself, empty wheelbarrow rumbling in front of her.

"Ah, Sophie, can I have a word? Is Maureen around? And Tig?"

"Oh, er… yes," Sophie's heart skipped a beat. "Maureen just went for her box of potions. Token Bay seems to have knocked himself and broken the skin a bit. Tig will be in the upstairs room, I think. They've just finished."

Fiona smiled gently. "Sophie. Your face?"

Sophie's eyes widened. She opened her mouth to speak but no words came out.

Maureen appeared, placed her wooden box at her feet and stood at Sophie's side. "She was hit by a whip. That Jameson chap. He was beating his horse."

"I…I just got in the way. Sort of."

Fiona smiled, and winced as her headache pounded.

"I know what happened. And it's OK, no-one's in trouble. But I need you both to come with me. To pay a visit to Jameson."

"Oh, I don't know, Fiona, I mean…" Sophie's voice broke off. She looked to Maureen, afraid to refuse but not wishing to see the man again.

"Don't worry, I don't mean you need to speak to him. I'll do the talking. We're going to fetch the horse."

"The horse? Oh, that's… oh fantastic."

"Maureen, can you drive the old horse box? Sophie, you can come along in case we need you to… persuade our Mr Jameson it's the right thing to do to let us have his horse."

"So, has he sold him to you then?" Maureen asked, though she thought she already knew the answer.

"Not yet."

Tig came to the bottom of the steps and, seeing Fiona talking with the girls, he tried to slip round to the horse walker without being seen.

"Ah, Tig!"

"Yes, Mrs Weston." Tig came over sheepishly, a terrified smile fixed on his face. He covered the knuckles on his right hand. Fiona glanced at his hands and raised her eyebrows.

"Well, it was like this you see…"

"Tig, it's fine. Really. I heard what happened." Her voice was uncharacteristically quiet as she explained the plan. "We're going over to Jameson's to fetch the horse. I'm not having the poor thing abused any more.

We should only be an hour or so. Can you finish mucking out and keep John from asking too many questions till we get back?"

Tig nodded. "I'll do my best, Mrs Weston. How long will you be?"

"We'll be back with the horse as soon as you've finished the mucking out! We'll leave right away."

"Oh, and can you put some of this on Token Bay's near side hock? He seems to have caught it on something and just broken the skin a bit." Maureen bent over her box, her hand hovering over the bottles and jars. She picked up a white jar and wiped the label on her jeans. "Ah, here it is. Aloe Vera Gel. Might sting a bit, but it'll be gone by tomorrow with a good dollop of that on."

"Sure." Tig smiled. Maureen smiled back.

"Right. Let's go. It's just the other side of Henton, so we shouldn't be long. I'll get the keys."

**

"So, you see, Mr Jameson, you really would be doing us a favour letting us have the horse. With Joe being unable to gallop for the foreseeable future, we need something steady to go round with Malé when owners are considering using him for their mares. It makes such a difference to see him in action."

"Well, I wasn't really looking to sell him yet, but…"

"Maureen here would be able to take him around our course, you see, and when she's not available it

262

would be…. Sophie." Fiona smiled slightly, her gaze steady.

The uncomfortable smile fell from Ron Jameson's face, replaced by a flash of fear, then the uncomfortable smile again.

Fiona said nothing but held his gaze until he sniffed miserably.

"Well, he's no racehorse but…. If you think you can make use of him, then… well, what can I say? It would be a pleasure, Mrs Weston."

"That's marvellous. I can assure you he'll have the best of homes with us. As you know, we have plenty of room, and all our horses are looked after properly. A good routine and lots of kindness."

Jameson pursed his lips. "In that case, we'd better discuss the price."

"Oh, I think a long-term loan would be more suitable. That way you still own the horse, but we'd look after him, keep an eye on him for you."

"Oh, but.."

"Unless you'd rather discuss yesterday's little incident with the police, Mr Jameson? I'm really not pleased that someone assaulted a member of my staff when they were having a day out. But if that's the way it has to be…" Fiona stood up to leave.

"Are you threatening me?"

"Not at all, Mr Jameson. I'm just giving you an opportunity to make us an offer we can't refuse. And then we can leave the matter behind us. Least said, soonest mended, as they say."

Jameson thought for a moment, tight lipped. "Alright. As long as it's the last I hear of it. And that bloody horse!"

"Of course. I think it's for the best. We have the horse box outside. If you can just show us where he is, we'll take him now."

Jameson led them through the house to the back porch. "He's in the second field on the right. Head collar outside the stable."

"Thank you." Fiona and Maureen made their way out. The door slammed behind them.

***

"Look Joe, the horse box is back. Do you think it's another mare?"

Joe raised his head from the grass in our small paddock and watched as the old vehicle made its way slowly along the track. He sniffed as it passed. "That's not a mare, Malé."

"Oh. No. I wonder who it is then."

"We'll find out soon enough," Joe dropped his head and continued nibbling the short grass, which had had the sun on it all morning and now tasted sweet.

Joe and me were out in the small paddock, as we were for a while each day now. Joe's leg had healed well, but he was only allowed to walk the short way from our cages and back. No running for a while. At first, Sophie and Maureen stayed in the paddock with us, holding the long ropes attached to our headcollars, and only in the small part which was fenced off from

Finn and Quest's summer field. It was much too small to gallop, and soon we were left there to graze together on our own for a short while, before we were taken back.

This time the horse who had just arrived was in the spare cage at the far end of the block. He stood at the back, warily eyeing everyone who went past. He was as tall as Joe and me, but more heavily built. His coat was grey, with dapples along his sides and quarters. Sophie and Maureen stopped to let us introduce ourselves as we passed.

Sophie leaned over the half door for a moment. The horse turned his head towards us but stayed where he was.

"It's OK, Pink. It's all going to be OK. No-one's going to beat you ever again," she said, and she turned and led Joe back into his stable.

Pastures New

"So, you see Miss Jones, we really can't lend based on the figures you've provided. It would just be too high risk."

"I see." Sophie stared at her folder on the bank manager's desk, graphs and figures covered the page.

"My advice would be to do some serious saving and come back when you have more collateral."

"Save? How much? Roughly."

"At least another ten thousand pounds. And you'd also need to reduce the size of your project somewhat. So you'd be in the market for a smaller farm."

"Ten thousand pounds? I'm a groom. That would take me till I'm seventy."

The manager smiled, sadly. "I'm very sorry."

Sophie sighed. She got up to leave.

"Have you thought about renting? As long as you can generate the income to cover the outgoings that might be a better option."

"Yes. I mean, no, I didn't think of that. But I will. Thank you." She took her folder and huddled it to her chest as she made her way out of the stuffy office and into the Autumn sunshine. Some wizened brown leaves blew past, blown by the traffic. An orange plastic bag followed them, whirling crazily until it came to rest in the gutter. Sophie gazed across the busy street for a moment, then sighed as she made her way to the bus stop to begin her journey home.

Later that day Sophie, Tig and Maureen sat in the pub discussing the options.

"So, did he have any ideas about getting ten grand, then?" Maureen sat back in her chair and placed her drink carefully back on the beer mat.

"No. Nothing. Just suggested renting instead" Sophie answered, miserably.

"Renting? How would that work?"

"I don't know. I've never thought about it really. I mean, some of the horses would be paid for, but I'd have to keep the yard full to make sure I could pay rent."

"Hmmm..." Maureen looked up at the hunting scene print on the wall above the fireplace. "But isn't that the same as having a mortgage? I mean, you'd have to pay that every month as well, right?"

"Yes, but at least you'd own the land at some point. Rent goes on forever. And you might not be able to organize it how you wanted."

"Have you spoken to Fiona or John about it?" Tig suggested.

"Of course not. Why do you say that?" Sophie and Maureen frowned.

"Well, hear me out. If you had some land and barns, you could take the youngsters off their hands until they were ready to go into training. And there's retired horses, like Quest and Finn. Maybe even Joe. If you offered that kind of thing, you could take in just a couple of rehabs at a time, until you were established."

Maureen looked interested. "That's not a bad idea. And you'd just be doing the same things as you do here, just at your own place."

268

"And I'm sure there are other racing yards that want that kind of service for their youngstock. You might be inundated! People are always saying how well mannered the horses are that come out of Weston's. Some of that's down to you, you know."

Sophie smiled at her friends. "Thanks. I know you're trying to help. Let me have a think. I might just be wanting the impossible." She stared into the bottom of her empty glass.

"Another drink." Maureen said firmly.

***

John finished the last mouthful of lasagne, reached for the bottle of Chardonnay, filling his glass then stretching over to fill Fiona's. She put her hand over it.

"No. No thanks. No more for me."

John stared at her. "Are you sure?" He checked the label. "It's a nice wine, this."

Fiona smiled. "No thanks."

"OK. More for me then!" John sloshed some more into his glass and took a mouthful. "So, as I was saying, we'll have eight, possibly nine new horses in the spring through the syndicate, which means we'll have fewer to sell next year, but a better income overall. And more runners, so more chance of winners…"

"John…"

"It was a pretty good decision going with Middletons. They seem to have cornered a new

269

market on shared ownership. Frank Jones had six last year and he's up to eight now…"

"John…"

"Seems to be the next new thing …

"John! For godsake will you be quiet!"

John put his glass down swiftly and looked at his wife. Fiona looked at her plate, half eaten sheets of pasta, cold and forlorn strewn across it.

"Is something up? Are you OK?"

"Yes. No. I don't know."

"That's not much to go on," John replied, smiling gently. "Come on, what's on your mind? We'll easily manage a few extra horses. It's not that is it?"

"No, of course not. It's…." Fiona paused for a moment, then half turned and reached into the bottom drawer pulling out a slim piece of white plastic. She held in in her hands for a second, then passed it across the table to her husband. "I'm pregnant."

***

"So, you see Miss Jones, the property has great potential for upgrading…. All original features and a nice size for keeping warm in the winter." The estate agent ducked under the low beam as he led Sophie, Maureen and Tig into the kitchen area from the yard outside. The grey flagstones were marked and worn, the huge white sink chipped, the tap dripped and a single naked bulb hung over the old wooden table. A faded tea towel hung over the rail of the Aga. Dust hung in the air as they moved on to the lounge. Sophie moved the heavy orange curtain aside.

"Oh look! Just look!" Maureen glanced up from where she was peeking under the white sheets to reveal an old sofa with a print of large flowers.

"Oh. That's gorgeous!" The three friends stared out of the window. A cloud, chased away by the brisk Autumn breeze passed by and sunlight flooded the valley. The trees were all but bare with the last few leaves of red or gold clinging to slender twigs, the grass bright after the rain, the hedgerows wild and bright with berries.

"A rainbow! That's got to be a good sign."

"Of course, there's a lot to do," the estate agent interrupted, "but as per the particulars, there's a range of machinery included in the tenancy, on top of the seventeen acres. And, of course, the contents of the house, which may or may not be of use…" His voice tailed off as Maureen glanced at the ancient furniture and raised her eyebrows at him.

They climbed the steep stairs to the upper floor. Two bedrooms, a tiny bathroom with a musty shower curtain and a huge oak wardrobe on the landing completed their tour.

"Let's hope there's no skeletons in that," Tig murmured.

As they passed through the lounge again and out into the sunshine, Sophie paused, looking back up the road towards Lower Barn Farm where she could just see Malé and Joe in their tiny paddock, heads down, nibbling round each front leg in turn as they made their way slowly across the grass.

She turned to the estate agent and smiled.

"It's lovely," she said. "Just what we were looking for."

"It's perfect, we'll take it!" Tig said.

Sophie opened her mouth and closed it again. "Um. Perhaps we should talk about it first?" she whispered to Tig.

"And let someone else have it? No. This is it Soph. It's right next to Westons, just the right size. And within budget. We could look for months and something like this wouldn't come up again. We can manage the work between us, and there's hardly anything to do to have it ready for the horses." He turned to the estate agent who was smiling politely, looking from one to the other.

"We'll take it and I'll have the deposit and the first month's rent in your account as soon as we've signed the papers."

"Certainly, Mr MacCauley. I'll have all the checks done and get everything ready. You'll need to come into the office, both of you, but it shouldn't take more than a couple of days, and then you can think about moving in."

He beamed as he shook their hands, nodding and thinking of his monthly bonus for getting a property let he'd been convinced no-one would want, with the house barely habitable and eight miles from the nearest shop. He nodded finally and got back into his car, waving as he left, clipboard and papers on the passenger seat, smiling to himself.

"Well. You did it." Maureen said. "Now we just have to tell John and Fiona."

A new home

"Tig! Tig," Sophie called from the lounge, pulling the rubber gloves from her hands and picking up the mop and bucket. Tig appeared in the doorway.

"Come and look at this," he beckoned excitedly, disappearing towards the stable block. Sophie smiled, set down her bucket by the sink and made her way across the cobbled yard to the first stable block.

"Here, look, press this. Go on!" Tig pointed towards the shiny silver bowl in the corner of the stable with his spanner.

"It's not going to explode is it?"

"I don't think so. Go on. Check it out!"

Sophie looked carefully at the bowl, pressed the lever and jumped back as fresh water spilled out into the bowl and onto the brick floor. "It's a bit fierce!"

"Yeah, I'll have to adjust it, but it's pretty good for half an hour's work, don't you think? No more running about with buckets to keep the horses in water," he smiled proudly.

"It's fantastic. Now can you work the same magic on the tap in the bathroom?"

"Oh that. You're so demanding," he teased. "Ben's coming over at the weekend to help me with that. I don't want to risk another flood."

"Ben the plumber, you mean?"

"No, he's a gynaecologist but it can't be that difficult," Tig replied.

Sophie laughed. "He'd better pop over to Weston's when he's done here then. His services might be needed pretty soon."

"Yeh, how long has she got?"

"Another three weeks, if things go to plan."

"They'd better do, or Fiona won't be best pleased."

"Babies turn up when they're ready, you can't always tell what they're about to do."

Tig smiled. "Do you think…."

"What?" Sophie pushed a stray lock of hair from her face.

"Do you think, one day we might…you know."

"What?" Sophie smiled coyly.

"You know what." Tig pulled her close to him. "One day, we might have a baby of our own."

"Hmmm," Sophie said, "if we have hot water and some form of heating I might consider it at some point."

"Better get Ben round ASAP then."

"Soph! What do you want me to do with these?" Maureen came out of the kitchen, her arms full of old rolls of wallpaper, some torn, most faded, all of them dusty.

"Ooh let's have a look. Might save us a few quid."

"You know Marcia's sorting the décor, Soph, you don't have to rough it with this stuff." They opened one of the rolls. It was brown with big beige flowers with orange centres.

"Hmmm… it might match the curtains…" Sophie held her head on one side, pretending to consider the wallpaper.

"Soph, if you want this putting up you can get someone else to do it. It's hideous. I'm putting them in the skip."

A small red car pulled onto the yard. The driver parked carefully next to the van Tig had borrowed and Marcia got out, looking elegant even in overalls. Her pink scarf tied loosely round her neck, fluttering briefly in the breeze. Maureen smiled and hugged her, Marcia kissed her cheek.

"Hello, it looks like I arrived at just the right time. You weren't seriously going to consider putting that old stuff on the walls were you?"

Sophie laughed. "Nope. Not when I can get good advice and some proper professional help." She hugged Marcia.

"I brought food!"

"Oh, thank god, my hero. I'm starving." Maureen said.

"And cake!" Marcia opened her boot and got out two carrier bags.

"I'll put the kettle on then."

Inside the farmhouse kitchen they pulled the heavy chairs around the old wooden table, newly scrubbed and oiled. The aga shone blue, a fresh tea towel over the polished rail, heating the water and warming the room at the same time. Tig brought another couple of logs inside and topped up the burner in the lounge as the women set out the sandwiches, warmed the brown teapot, poured milk from the blue striped jug into mugs, filling the kitchen with happy chatter.

"So, how is the world of interior décor, Marcia?" Tig pulled the plate of sandwiches towards him and grabbed a couple, setting them onto his plate and plonking himself in a chair.

"Oh, it's all good fun, you know," she said, tossing her blond ponytail over her shoulder. "I've managed to swing a pretty splendid contract with Colmans."

"Oh, the pub chain?" Tig said, stuffing his mouth with cheese and pickle sandwich.

"Er… gastro-pub, if you don't mind, Mister Mac!" she replied, tutting and rolling her eyes. "I've got to create a new design that's family friendly, yet elegant, reflecting the chain's aspirations to appeal to families with mid-range budgets. There's one in Tipton, not far from here."

"Ooh," said Sophie, "can we come and have a look when it's done?"

"Course," Marcia replied, "as long as I can use some before and after pictures of your new rural idyll in my portfolio."

"Do you think it'll be that nice when it's done?" Maureen looked doubtful.

"Maureen. Of course it will!" Marcia said firmly. "Now, I've got the books in the car, so you can see the sort of things we can do. Make a start on the cake while I get them in."

She got up, Maureen helped herself to a slice of Victoria sponge and passed the plate across to Tig.

"Not for me thanks. Two more rides this weekend."

"Oh, yes," said Maureen, mouth full of cake, "you can't afford to be over the weight. What's the prize money for this one?"

"Ten grand."

"Crikey! You're going up in the world." She moved the plate away from him. "Shame you don't get to keep it all."

"Too right. But it should cover the new fencing in the top paddock. The sooner we get that sorted, the sooner we can get the horses in."

"You just need to make sure you win."

"John's promised he'll put me up on Tidal Reef every time he runs this year. So at some point…"

"At some point this place can start earning you two some money. Where are you going to put Joe and Malé?"

"Oh, the first paddock, next to the house, And the oldies, at least for the Summer, and Pink."

"Poor old boy." Maureen stopped eating and gazed out of the window for a moment then returned to her Victoria sponge.

"Where were you thinking of? Pink can be quite hard to pull off you know, especially in these smaller types of room, although it all depends on the shade, of course." Marcia rejoined them, plonked some heavy samples books on the table and adjusted her scarf.

"Ew, pink," said Sophie.

"She meant the horse Marse," Maureen replied.

Marcia tittered. "Oh right. The horse. Why didn't I think of that?"

"Right, I'll leave you ladies with the interior décor and get on with my plumbing." Tig stood up, kissing Sophie's cheek as he passed on his way out, with his large white mug half full of tea.

"What do you think Fiona will call the baby?" Sophie mused.

"Something solid I expect. With their dad's names as spares."

"So it's definitely a boy then?"

"I don't reckon it would dare be a girl."

"What's wrong with being a girl?" Marcia asked.

"That inheritance thing," Maureen answered, knowingly.

"But Fiona inherited Lower Barn Farm."

"Of course. You've known her since college, haven't you?" Sophie remembered.

"Yes, we were there at the same time, over in Stow. We weren't in any lectures together, of course, Fiona studied different stuff to me, but we all shared the rest of the facilities and we hung around with the same crowd. We all thought she'd be the last to get married and have a family. But..." Marcia thought for a moment. "There's only her and Gabby who have had babies so far, out of about 10 of us."

"Well, I'm pretty glad she did. We're getting as much work as we can handle, now John's getting more horses in and Fiona's out of action for a while."

"It's all worked out brilliantly," Maureen answered, gazing briefly at her girlfriend, then back at her best friend. "For all of us."

About the Author

Sabrina has been around horses since she was nine years old. She bought her first horse in 2004, who is now retired and spends his time with his two friends in a field in Leicestershire.

Sabrina is a member of several equine learning groups, and lectures on genetic diseases which can go undiagnosed and cause pain to those horses who are affected.

This is Sabrina's first novel, and she is now writing a screenplay as well as her weekly radio sketches which she also performs.